Things just got worse. . . .

We were losing the battle to keep the sailboat afloat.

"Ian?" Talia stuck her head into the cabin. She looked serious and pale. "You better come up here."

Both Stuart and Talia had stopped what they were doing and were staring at the water. At first, in the glare of the sun, I didn't see anything. Then I saw long dark torpedo shapes moving rapidly under the water. A gray dorsal fin cut through the surface.

Sharks. . . .

AGAINST THE ODDS™: Shark Bite

By Todd Strasser

From Minstrel Books
Published by Pocket Books

TODD STRASSER
AGAINST THE ODDS™

SHARK BITE

A
MINSTREL®
BOOK

Published by POCKET BOOKS
New York   London   Toronto   Sydney   Tokyo   Singapore

A MINSTREL PAPERBACK *Original*

 A Minstrel Book published by
POCKET BOOKS, a division of Simon & Schuster Inc.
1230 Avenue of the Americas, New York, NY 10020

TM and Copyright © 1998 by Todd Strasser

ISBN: 0-671-02309-8

First Minstrel Books printing October 1998

10 9 8 7 6 5 4 3 2 1

A MINSTREL BOOK and colophon are registered trademarks of Simon & Schuster Inc.

Front cover illustration by Franco Accornero

Printed in the U.S.A.

To Noah and Joshua Strone

SHARK
BITE

1

"You don't want to sail on her today, shark bait," Pops said.

Sitting on the dock, I looked up at him. I was twelve and a half, and Pops looked like he was a hundred. Well, seventy-five at the very least. His skin was wrinkled from way too many years working in the sun. He walked with a limp, and his clothes were stained and tattered.

"You're darn right," I said and took a bite out of a chocolate glazed doughnut.

The deep lines in Pops's forehead deepened. I guess my answer must have thrown him. Here I was in the early morning, sitting on the dock with my duffel bag, scarfing down a box of doughnuts and a container of orange juice for breakfast. Moored to the dock beside me was this beautiful red-hulled sailboat with the stupid name of the *Big Bucks*. To the casual observer it must have looked as if I couldn't wait to go sailing.

"Ain't you sailing with the Greens?" Pops asked.

"But that doesn't mean I *want* to go," I answered.

"Yeah, well, I'm sure you got your reasons," Pops said with a snort. "But here's a reason you ain't got. You sail this morning, and in about twenty-four hours you're gonna find yourself in the middle of some weather you ain't never dreamed of."

I frowned. The early-morning air in the marina was practically still. The flags on the sailboats around us drooped lifelessly. Not only that, but I'd checked the weather maps on the Internet at school the day before. Except for a tropical depression forming off Cape Verde, Africa, the radar in the Western Hemisphere was clear.

And Cape Verde, Africa, was an awful long way from Galveston Bay in the Gulf of Mexico.

"Says who?" I asked.

"Says my arthritis." Pops held up his left hand. It was gnarled and scarred, the fingers bent and the joints swollen to twice their nor-

2

mal size. "Says sixty years of shrimping in these waters till these hands got so bad they couldn't hold a net no more."

I had no reason to believe the old man's prediction. Then again, I had no reason *not* to believe him, either. Pops had spent his life on the water and probably knew ten times more about sea weather than the computer geeks who sat in a windowless room somewhere reading satellite data.

I looked back down the dock—past the dozens of expensive sailboats owned by millionaires who used them maybe three times a year—and then only on sunny, warm days when the wind was just right. Back down there was the Crystal Bay Yacht Club restaurant, and up on the porch sat my sister, Talia, having breakfast with Buck Green and his jerky son, Stuart.

Buck Green was a divorced, big-shot tax lawyer. I didn't know his son Stuart very well, but I'd heard that he was your basic spoiled, rich tenth grader. Stuart just happened to be crazy about my sister, Talia, who was in ninth grade. Today was the first day of a two-week Easter vacation, and Mr. Green was taking Stuart, Talia, and me on a sailing trip to Cancun, Mexico.

When Talia first told me about the trip, I was

3

both excited and disappointed. I was excited because Talia and I had never been anywhere. Our dad died when we were young, and our mom worked two jobs to support us. Neither Talia nor I had traveled much, other than a couple of Christmas visits to an aunt's house in Tulsa, and a Mardi Gras weekend in New Orleans. Every piece of clothing Talia owned, she'd either made herself or bought with money earned from baby-sitting.

At the same time I was disappointed because it was hard to believe that Talia really liked Stuart. You had to believe that she only said yes to the invitation because it was a chance for her to travel.

And what was I doing there? Well, first off, Mom didn't want my sister to go on this sailing trip alone. So even though I was in seventh grade and a year and a half younger than Talia, I was sent along to chaperone. Second, Buck Green needed a crew for the trip across the Gulf, and as far as I knew, Stuart didn't know a jib from a mainsail. On the other hand, I'd been totally in love with the sea since the first time Mom took Talia and me to the beach on Galveston Island.

Being that I'm tall for my age and I lift weights, people tend to think I'm older than I actually am. One of my mom's friends worked in the yacht club office, and she'd helped me get jobs the past two summers on the yacht club dock pumping gas and running the launch that carried the club members to their moorings. That's how I'd gotten to know Stuart's father. More important, that's how Mr. Green had gotten to know me.

I guess I was known as someone who could be relied upon to be good crew when no one else was available. On my days off I sometimes filled in as a crewman on sailboats whose owners were always glad to have an extra hand along to help with mooring and winching up the mainsail. So that made me perfect for the trip to Mexico. For my mother's sake I would keep an eye on my sister. For Mr. Green's sake I would do the grunt work.

And in return I'd get to go on my first overnight sailing trip, plus free room and board in Cancun. All in all, it wasn't a bad deal.

"So?" Pops was waiting for some kind of answer to his warning on the weather.

"Gotta go, Pops," I said, and crumpled up the orange juice container.

"You'll be sorry, shark bait."

"Maybe," I replied.

5

2

Pops limped away down the dock mumbling to himself. Of course, he wasn't a yacht club member, just an old bum people felt sorry for. With those hands and that bad leg he hardly ever got out on the water anymore. Walking the docks was about as close as he got these days.

I looked back toward the yacht club restaurant and saw that the Greens and my sister were getting up. Breakfast was over. Half an hour ago they'd invited me to eat with them, but I couldn't quite see myself sitting at a linen-covered table sipping orange juice from a crystal glass and watching Stuart Green make dumb moon-eyes at my sister. So I'd begged off and eaten my doughnuts and drank my orange juice from its container by myself.

And now the trip was about to begin. I looked back down at the *Big Bucks* with an involuntary sense of envy. She was a beautiful sailboat. Her bright red hull and gold racing stripe didn't show a scratch. Her polished-steel rails glinted in the sun, and her brand-new Mylar sails were the best made. I couldn't imagine what she must have cost.

And the thought of rough weather didn't particularly worry me. From the radar atop the stern tower and the antennas on the mast, I could tell that she was equipped with enough electronics to sail any ocean in the world.

And compared to an ocean crossing, the eight-hundred-mile trip to Cancun would be a stroll in the park.

The Greens and Talia appeared at the beginning of the dock and started toward me. Talia was wearing jeans and a white blouse, her blond hair pulled back into a ponytail and that ever-present smile on her lips. Stuart loped along beside her, pushing a green cart loaded with overnight bags and cardboard boxes filled with groceries and other supplies. Ahead of them marched Buck Green, a tall, barrel-chested man who always took the lead in any group.

"How's she look, Ian?" Mr. Green asked me,

his always-loud voice booming over the morning quiet. It was more of a boast than a question. "She" was the *Big Bucks,* and both Mr. Green and I knew she looked beautiful.

"Pretty good, sir," I replied.

"Pretty good, huh?" Buck Green chuckled. "A heck of a lot better than anything you've ever sailed on."

And that pretty much set the tone for the trip. Buck Green was making sure I knew my place. Behind his jocular manner was a hard, boastful man who thought he was better than most everyone else. He wasn't the kind of person you'd want to do a serious ocean-crossing with, but he was probably okay for the trip from Galveston to Cancun.

Stuart and Talia arrived beside the sloop. Stuart stopped pushing the cart full of bags. "Get this stuff on board, Ian," he said.

I shot a quick glance at Talia to let her know I thought Stuart was a jerk for giving me orders. Talia lowered her eyes. She knew it.

Meanwhile, instead of taking hold of the railing and stepping carefully onto the sailboat, Stuart jumped off the dock and landed in the *Big Bucks* cockpit with a loud thud. It was the stunt of a show-off. And a dumb stunt, too, because it could have cracked the cockpit floor.

Even Mr. Green grimaced at the stupidity of his son's move.

Stuart reached over and offered his hand to my sister. "Come on, Talia, let me show you around."

Talia took Stuart's hand briefly and let him help her into the cockpit. He opened the companionway door, and they both went down into the cabin. Mr. Green stepped into the cockpit and followed them inside. I was left on the dock to unload the bags and carry them onto the boat.

By the time I finished getting the bags on, Buck Green had checked out the electronics.

"Let's get sailing," he said, coming back up to the cockpit. "You better get that stuff stowed below, Ian."

I paused just for a second, not because I resented taking orders—I'd known beforehand that I'd be expected to take plenty of them on this trip—but because I was wondering again about what Pops had said.

"You didn't hear anything about a storm coming up, did you?" I asked.

Buck Green shook his head. "The Gulf looked as clear as a whistle on the Weather Channel this morning. Why? Did you hear something?"

I thought about repeating Pops's warning, then decided against it. Who'd believe a warning from some old bum when every modern weather forecasting device in the Western Hemisphere was calling for a smooth trip?

"No." I shook my head. "Just making sure."

Then I picked up a box of groceries and headed belowdecks.

3

"Almost half a million dollars," Stuart was saying to Talia when I came belowdecks with the box of groceries. He clammed up when he saw me, but I was pretty sure he'd been bragging about how much the *Big Bucks* had cost. The price seemed staggering for a sailboat, but at the same time not surprising. I was pretty sure she was custom-built.

Certainly the main cabin looked it, with its burnished wood and built-in berths. And the galley looked expensive, too, with its gas cooktop and microwave oven, not to mention the small refrigerator and two-sink countertop. I opened the refrigerator and started to stow the perishables inside.

"Uh, let's go up top," Stuart immediately said

to Talia, as if he didn't want to be around her little brother. "I want to show you something cool."

Stuart stepped past without looking at me. But once again I caught Talia's eye. And once again my sister glanced away. She and Stuart went back up the companionway steps and through the door, back up to the cockpit. I continued to stow the groceries. A rumble shook the boat slightly as Mr. Green started the diesel engine. We would motor out into the bay, where we'd pick up some wind and start to sail.

The companionway door opened. Talia came back down the steps, carrying another box of groceries.

I looked up at her. "You don't have to do that."

"You think I should leave it for the cabin boy?" she replied with a wink as she kneeled down beside me and helped fill the refrigerator.

I grinned. "Hey, that's the price of passage. Besides, I bet Stuart's looking for you."

"Stuart's helping his father cast off," Talia replied.

I lowered my voice. "You sure you want to do this?"

"Which?" Talia asked. "Put away the groceries or sail to Cancun for two weeks?"

"What do you think?" I asked.

"I think this could be the most fun trip you and I have ever had," answered my sister.

"Even with Stuart?"

"He's not so bad," Talia said.

"Sheesh!" I muttered. "In that case, I'd hate to see what you think bad is."

"I'm serious, Ian," Talia said. "Just because he's rich doesn't make him a jerk."

"Did you see how he jumped off the dock and into the sailboat?" I asked.

My sister shrugged it off. "It's not a big deal. Boys are always showing off."

"Oh, yeah," I smirked. "I guess it's because you're so beautiful and they have to impress you."

Talia gave me a playful nudge and then headed back up to the cockpit. I wondered if she was right about it being a fun trip. The truth was, I'd never sailed more than five miles out into the Gulf of Mexico before. Not even far enough to be out of sight of the land. Maybe she was right. This just might turn out to be the trip of a lifetime.

4

A little while later, out in the gulf, the day turned beautiful and breezy. The sun was high. Except for a few cotton ball clouds here and there, the sky was clear. The Mylar mainsail and jib filled with wind, and the *Big Bucks* cut smartly through the gulf swells.

I sat in the cockpit with Mr. Green, who was at the wheel. Like a lot of large sailboats equipped to sleep six or eight persons, the cockpit was built above the cabin instead of behind it. They called it a center cockpit design, and it helped the sailor see ahead. Over the cockpit a low green canopy provided shade.

From the cockpit I could see Stuart and Talia up in the bow, sunbathing. Stuart was wearing a diving knife strapped to his right calf.

"Ever been to Mexico before?" Mr. Green asked me.

"No, sir."

"You'll like it," Mr. Green said. "Great beaches, good food. I noticed you and your sister brought snorkel equipment. Done much snorkeling?"

"Some," I replied.

"Where?"

"Just around Galveston."

"Galveston?" Buck Green grinned. "What'd you see? A whole lot of sand and a couple of flounder?"

"When the water was clear," I replied. "Most times the water's so murky you can't even see that."

"Well, just wait till you see some of my favorite reefs off Quintana Roo," Mr. Green said. "Make sure you remind me to stop when we get down there. You'll think you were in your own private aquarium."

I appreciated the suggestion. It was weird, though, how everything Mr. Green said made it seem as if we were entering some special world that only he had access to. As if those reefs off Quintana Roo really were his.

"Hey, Dad! Look!" Up on the bow Stuart was pointing off the starboard side. About three hundred yards away a fisherman was battling what appeared to be a really large fish.

"Go below and get my binoculars," Mr. Green told me.

I ducked into the cabin and returned quickly with the binoculars. They were, of course, a totally spectacular pair, larger than any I had ever seen, and with auto-focus.

"Take the wheel, son," Mr. Green said. He took the binoculars and stood in the cockpit. I took the wheel.

"Oh, yeah." A smile appeared on Mr. Green's lips as he looked through the binoculars. "That good old boy's got himself a big one. Here, Ian, take a look."

He handed the glasses to me. Even though I really wanted to see the fish, I also didn't want to give up the wheel. The *Big Bucks* handled so smoothly, like nothing I'd ever sailed before. But taking the glasses, I was amazed by how close and clear the image became. The man fighting the fish was strapped into a fighting chair in the back of a sport-fishing cruiser, his heavy black rod bent severely. Huddled around him were a bunch of other men. One of them had a rifle. Fifteen feet behind the boat the water boiled and turned white as the fish thrashed and fought just beneath the surface.

"What's the rifle for?" I asked, handing the binoculars back to Mr. Green.

"Shark," he answered.

With my bare eyes I could just make out the man shouldering the rifle and leaning out over the gunnel.

Bang! A shot rang out, and then another. The roiling water behind the fishing boat began to grow calm and clear.

"Got him," Mr. Green said, watching through the binoculars with one hand and steering with the other.

On the fishing boat one of the men reached out with a long gaff and slowly began to pull the shark in.

"Phew, that's one big fish," Mr. Green said.

"What are they doing, Dad?" Stuart called from the bow.

"Looks like they're gonna get a rope around the tail and haul it up," Mr. Green called back.

Sure enough, the mate looped a rope around the shark's tail and then started to winch it up with a block and tackle next to the fishing boat's cabin. As the fish came out of the water, Mr. Green let out a slow whistle and handed the binoculars back to me.

I had never seen a fish so big, at least not one that wasn't stuffed and hanging in a restaurant somewhere. It was definitely a shark, brownish in color with short vertical stripes.

"What kind is it?" Stuart called from the bow.

"Tiger shark," Mr. Green called back. "Probably five hundred pounds."

"Cool!" Stuart called back.

"Yup," Mr. Green agreed in a low voice only I could hear. "Cool as long as you don't find yourself in the water with one."

5

The rest of the morning was a perfect sail. By midmorning we'd lost sight of the Texas coast and were surrounded on all sides by rolling blue-green sea and deep blue sky. Buck Green let me take the wheel a couple of times. But when Mr. Green asked his son to do the same, Stuart said he wasn't interested.

And I could see why. About the only thing Stuart was interested in was staying close to Talia. I was almost embarrassed for the guy. He was so awkward and obvious in the way he kept trying to accidentally rub her shoulder or take her hand. Talia responded with unending patience, always skirting his touch and making light of it with a laugh. It was just hard for me to believe that Stuart wasn't getting the message.

About the only time Stuart helped was when he and Talia went below and made sandwiches for lunch. The four of us sat in the cockpit under the green canvas canopy and ate together.

"What do we do at night?" Talia asked.

"Keep sailing," Mr. Green said. "We'll take watches. Two hours on, four hours off."

"Is it safe to sail at night?" asked my sister.

"Out here in the Gulf, sure," answered Mr. Green. "We've got radar. There's no reefs or shoals to worry about. The only thing you have to watch for are other ships, but you'll see their lights and have plenty of time to steer around them."

"Sounds pretty cool," said Stuart. "Suppose Talia and I take the first watch?"

"Fine," said his father. "Only, make sure you pay attention to sailing."

Stuart responded with a goofy grin, and Talia turned a little red. I prayed it wasn't something she really had to worry about.

The afternoon passed comfortably. The only excitement came when Stuart came running back down the deck toward the cockpit yelling "Sharks!"

I had the wheel. Mr. Green was dozing in the sun. The yelling caught him by surprise and he jumped.

"Swimming along the bow!" Stuart cried breathlessly.

"What?" His father scowled.

I looked toward the bow and saw Talia holding her stomach and laughing as she pointed over the side. A pair of porpoises were racing along the bow wake.

Mr. Green frowned at his son. "Can't you tell the difference?"

"Well, I thought they were sharks," Stuart stammered. "I mean, all I saw was the fins cutting through the water. It looked like sharks."

"Next time make sure before you go running around alarming everyone, Chicken Little." Mr. Green's tone toward his son was cutting. "Porpoises aren't even fish, for Pete's sake. In fact, they're known for having intelligence that rivals that of humans, if you know what I mean."

Stuart's eyes darted at me and his face turned red. I was surprised that Mr. Green would cut down his own son so publicly.

Stuart didn't come near the cockpit for the rest of the afternoon. Later, he and Talia cooked dinner. Once again we all ate under the canopy. A sheet of thin clouds had started to cover the sky, and I was disappointed when the sunset became a faint blur of red sun surrounded by gray.

After dinner Talia and Stuart went below to watch TV. Mr. Green stayed above to sail. I was doing the dinner dishes in the galley when I glanced over at the chart table and noticed that the barometer readings had dropped from earlier in the day.

I finished the dishes and went back up to the cockpit. By now it was dark. The air felt heavy and damp. I couldn't tell whether it was because night had fallen or something else. With the stars hidden behind the clouds, it seemed very dark. The *Big Bucks* had red and green running lights in the bow, as well as a light in the cockpit. A bright beacon shined from the top of the mast. Mr. Green must have turned on the radar, because in the cockpit the radar screen glowed green.

"Kind of dark, huh?" I said as I joined Mr. Green in the cockpit.

"Not to worry," Buck Green replied. "We've still got two or three miles visibility, and this." He pointed at the radar screen. "Any boat bigger than a dingy comes within a mile of us and we'll know it."

"I noticed the barometer was falling," I said.

Mr. Green raised an eyebrow and gave me a surprised look. It wasn't much, just enough to let me know that he was impressed that I'd noticed.

22

"It sure has," he agreed. "Looks like we may have a little tropical depression ahead. Might turn into a squall. But the winds have stayed pretty steady. I don't imagine there's much to be concerned about."

I gazed quietly off the stern, feeling the damp salt breeze in my face. Because it was so dark out, here and there in the boat's wake I could see slight bursts of glow-stick green phosphorescence. For a while I just stared at it in wonder. Until that moment it was something I'd only read about in books.

"Ahem." Mr. Green cleared his throat. "I don't know if you're tired or not, but you might want to go belowdecks and get some rest before your watch."

I knew I probably wouldn't be able to sleep, but I went belowdecks anyway. Talia and Stuart were down there in the main cabin watching TV. Stuart didn't look happy when I joined them, but it wasn't as if I had any place else to go. As I watched the TV, I noticed that the *Big Bucks* was gradually heeling over as if picking up more wind. At one point I heard footsteps on the deck above and wondered if Mr. Green was adjusting the sails because of the increasing blow.

Around midnight Mr. Green came down and said it was Talia's and Stuart's watch.

23

"I've put her on autopilot," Mr. Green told his son. "You might want to throw on a rain jacket. It's getting a little damp up there."

Stuart and Talia opened one of the lockers and pulled out yellow rain jackets, then headed up the companionway.

"And one other thing," Mr. Green said. "Make sure you both have safety harnesses on."

Stuart looked puzzled. "Is something wrong?"

Mr. Green shook his head. "No, it's just a precaution at night. One of you accidentally slips off the deck, it won't be easy to find you in the dark."

Stuart and Talia headed up the companionway stairs to the cockpit.

Mr. Green turned to me. "You're on from two A.M. until four A.M., Ian. You better get some rest. Stuart will wake you when it's your turn."

"How's the weather?" I asked.

"Uh . . ." Mr. Green hesitated. "I'd say it's in a slow decline."

"But still nothing to worry about?"

"Right," confirmed Mr. Green. "Still nothing to worry about."

6

My sister and I had berths in the main cabin. Stuart and his father would sleep in the forward cabin. Each berth was basically a long narrow couch. To insure that you didn't roll off in the middle of the night, the berth had a bunk board on a hinge. When the bunk board was raised, you were enclosed on three sides. It was like lying in a coffin with the top open.

I did sleep, but not for long and not very well. With the sailboat heeling sharply, I was basically wedged into a corner of the berth. Around two A.M. I felt a hand shake my shoulder. I looked up into Stuart's face.

"Your turn," he said with a yawn. "The autopilot's on. Just make sure she stays on a heading of 280 degrees. And don't forget the harness."

Bleary and only half-awake, I crawled out of the berth and stumbled through the galley, using the overhead handrails to steady myself. Talia was already in her berth. I have to admit I was surprised that Stuart knew what our heading was. Maybe the guy knew more about sailing than he let on.

As I grew less groggy, I became aware that the *Big Bucks* was heeled over sharply. Going through the galley was like walking on a slanted floor in a fun house.

When I opened the companionway door, the night air hit me like a slap. It was colder and wetter than I'd expected, and the wind was blowing hard. It wasn't until I took the wheel that I realized that the *Big Bucks* was heeling as much as twenty degrees. With the wind blowing that hard Mr. Green had taken down the jib. Those were the footsteps I remembered hearing over the cabin while I'd watched TV.

I slid on the safety harness, pulled it tight, and made sure it was buckled to the cabin rail. I couldn't help feeling a little nervous. In the dark without the moon or stars, the visibility was lousy. You stared ahead at the black sea with no sense of how far you were seeing. It could have been a hundred feet or a thousand yards. It was impossible to tell. The good news was that the winds were steady, and the *Big*

Bucks was a big enough boat to cut through the growing waves. But I knew this wind was a recent development. The longer it blew, the bigger the waves would become.

Still, Stuart and Talia had been out here just a few minutes ago, and it didn't seem to bother them. If anything, this weather should have freaked Stuart out long before it freaked me. I checked the radar. The sea around us was clear. As long as I kept a heading of 280, things should be fine.

The wind continued to pick up for the next two hours, and it started to rain. I found foul-weather gear in a cockpit locker and pulled it on. The rain was coming down at a sharp angle. In fact, there were gusty moments when it seemed to be raining sideways. The seas were growing choppy, too. The spray off the tops of the waves was adding to the sheets of moisture blowing through the air. The *Big Buck's* bow rose and plunged as it fought through the deepening troughs between the waves.

The truth was, I'd never sailed in such rough weather, and the fact that it was night only made it worse. A couple of times, after a particularly big wave or strong gust, I thought about going below and alerting Mr. Green to the deteriorating weather. But each time I thought of it, I'd check the hour and then decide that it wouldn't be long until it was Mr. Green's watch again. Why not let him sleep a little longer? No doubt, Stuart's father would appreciate it.

So I decided to wait.

It was blowing and raining hard at 4:10 A.M. when the companionway door opened and Mr. Green joined me in the cockpit. Stuart's father was wearing rain gear. He silently pulled on a safety harness. In the darkness and driving rain and sea spray, visibility was basically zero. The *Big Bucks* rose over the tops of waves, then crashed down in the troughs. Stuart's father checked the radar and the compass reading.

"Good." He grunted with a short nod. "Still on course."

I took that as a sign that things were okay. I unbuckled my safety harness from the cabin rail and started to reach for the companionway door, eager to get out of the wind and rain.

"Hold it," Mr. Green said. "Let's see if we can find out what we're in for." He flicked on the weather band radio.

The National Weather Service was forecasting a squall in the western Gulf. Small craft warnings had been posted. Gale-force winds, heavy rain, and wave heights of more than fif-teen feet were expected.

Mr. Green wiped the rain and sea spray off his face. "Looks like we're in for some heavy weather," he said.

He wasn't smiling.

7

I got a true sense of just how rough it had become when I tried to go belowdecks. The pitching of the sailboat made a challenge of each step. Holding the railings tightly, I stepped slowly, knowing that at any moment the boat could roll and I might be thrown across the cabin.

Down below I found Talia sitting up in her berth, bracing herself. Still wearing her clothes from the night before, she bit her lip and looked scared.

"What's going on?" she asked.

"We've hit some bad weather." I braced myself with one hand and tried to get out of the wet rain gear with the other. "Seen Stuart?"

"He must be in there." Talia pointed toward the forward cabin door.

Just then the sailboat dipped sharply, as if it was sledding down the face of a huge wave. Talia and I had to grab the overhead handrail to keep from tumbling into the bow. The pillows from the berths slid forward and a plastic cup on the countertop fell to the cabin floor and rolled into the bulkhead.

The sailboat seemed to hit the trough, straighten out, and then veer sharply to the starboard side. Still holding the railing, Talia and I were practically swung off our feet.

Crash! A wave hit us broadside, throwing the sailboat so far over that it felt for a moment as if she were lying on her side. A locker across the cabin from us burst open, spilling out rolled-up charts and navigation books. The cushions in my berth tumbled out and fell on Talia and me.

A moment later the *Big Bucks* righted herself. A sense of relief passed through me. Mr. Green had regained control of the sailboat. For a second it felt as if we'd been trapped in some out-of-control carnival ride. Luckily, Talia and I had managed to hang on. Otherwise we might both have been thrown across the cabin and hurt.

"What's the story?" Stuart pushed open the door between the main and forward cabins. He

31

was wearing a T-shirt and boxer shorts, and his voice sounded high and strained.

"We've hit a squall," I said.

"One second I was in my berth," Stuart said. "The next thing I knew, I was on the floor."

"You better put up your bunk board," I said.

"Forget it." Stuart shook his head and gestured back into the forward cabin. "I'm not staying alone in there."

There were four berths in the main cabin, so there was room for Stuart. Meanwhile, the *Big Bucks* felt as if she was back on course, albeit seesawing sharply as she rode up the face of waves and then slid down their backs.

"We might as well stay in our berths and ride this thing out," I said. "It's probably the safest place to be right now."

Bracing ourselves against the constant seesawing, we gathered up the cushions that had spilled out of the berths. Talia and Stuart got into their berths and secured their bunk boards to keep from rolling out. I had just started across the cabin to my own berth when the sailboat pitched sharply again, throwing me against the lockers.

Ow! I cracked my head hard on the wooden locker.

"Ian!" Talia gasped. "Are you okay?"

Grabbing the overhead railing with one

hand, I felt my head with the other. It throbbed painfully, but thankfully, there was no blood.

"Yeah," I answered. "I'm all right."

"Be careful," my sister admonished.

"Believe me, I'm trying." I managed to swing myself into my berth and pull up my bunk board. Now I was cradled in my own open-faced coffin.

Meanwhile, the sailboat continued to pitch and thrash as if we were on some bent-out-of-shape roller coaster.

"Good thing no one's getting seasick," Stuart commented from his berth.

"Are we going to be okay?" Talia asked.

"Sure," I replied, not wanting her to worry. The *Big Bucks* was sturdy and well-built. You really had to believe that it would take a lot more than some rough seas to do any damage to her.

8

Crash! For a second I was completely airborne. Then, with a sickening crunch, I slammed against the wall of my berth and was nearly spilled out onto the floor. From all around the boat came the sounds of things banging and cracking. It felt as if some giant had just plucked the *Big Bucks* out of the water and dropped it on the ground. We'd almost tipped upside down in the process. In sailing terms it was called a knockdown.

"Ian!" Talia cried from her berth.

"What was that?" Stuart cried. "Did we hit something?"

I waited a moment before answering. It sure felt as if we'd hit something. But now I wasn't so sure. Once again the sailboat seemed to right itself. We were still floating.

"I don't think we hit anything," I said. "I think something hit us."

"Another boat?" Stuart guessed.

"A wave," I said. "I have a feeling we just fell off the top of one."

"Off the top of a wave?" Talia repeated.

"It must have been huge," added Stuart.

In the cabin wall above my berth was a long, narrow window. Holding tightly, I stretched up and looked out. What met my eyes at first was a gray blur as driving rain and sea spume splashed against the glass outside. Long white streams of wind-blown sea foam seemed to be flying sideways.

Gradually I caught glimpses of huge gray waves. It was impossible to gauge their exact heights, but they dwarfed the sailboat. They were waves the size of houses, towering high above us each time we slid down into a trough.

The sight of them was dizzying. I felt the breath leave my lungs and refuse for a moment to come back. I'd never seen waves so big. Not even on TV.

Whoa! The sailboat rocked severely. The cabin filled with the sounds of loose items crashing. I peeked over the edge of the bunk board and looked out of my berth. The floor of the cabin was littered with books, plastic glasses, weather gear, and videocassettes.

More lockers must've spilled open in the knock-down. Meanwhile, the *Big Bucks* was rocking violently from side to side instead of seesawing forward through the waves. Being sideways in waves was the worse thing imaginable. No boat in the world, no matter what its size, could survive a beating like this for long without breaking apart.

Crash! Another wave hit us broadside, almost knocking the sailboat over. In the cabin everything became airborne again. More lockers burst open, showering us with clothes, cushions, cassettes, and books.

"What's going on?" Talia cried.

A sickening feeling swept through me. It wasn't seasickness, but the suspicion that there was no one at the helm of the *Big Bucks* anymore. She was drifting directionless in the storm.

And what about Mr. Green?

Crash! Another wave rocked the sailboat. Something was definitely wrong. If Mr. Green had control of the boat, we would have been running with the waves, not being struck repeatedly by them broadside. I wondered how long the sailboat could stand up to this beating before it broke in half or was simply swamped and sank.

"Why's this happening?" Stuart whimpered

fearfully. He seemed to be talking as much to himself as anyone else. "I don't understand it. Why's it doing this?"

"What should we do?" Talia asked.

I already knew the answer. One of us had to go up to the cockpit.

Crash! We were hit and rocked again. Loose tools and cans of food became missiles each time the sailboat heeled over, smashing and banging into everything. The inside of the boat would be destroyed, and someone badly hurt, if something wasn't done.

And done fast!

"Stop it!" Stuart cried out in terror as the boat rocked again.

Talia stared across the cabin at me with a terrified expression. It was becoming obvious who was going up to see what was wrong. It was the last thing in the world I wanted to do. But if I didn't do it, we might all be in terrible trouble. I unlatched my bunk board and swung my legs out.

"Where are you going?" Talia asked nervously.

"To see what's wrong," I answered.

Crash! Another wave hit the *Big Bucks*. I was dumped back into my berth and showered with cushions, cans, and other junk.

"Ian?" Talia called when the sailboat righted itself again.

"It's okay." I dug my way out of the junk and started to pull on some rain gear. It took three times as long as usual but I finally got it on and a life jacket over it. Over that I strapped on a safety harness.

In a rueful moment of black humor I realized it was a good thing the lockers had spilled open. Otherwise it would have been a lot harder to find all this stuff.

With one hand on each of the overhead rails, I stood up in the main cabin.

"Should one of us come with you?" Talia asked, poking her head up over her bunk board.

I glanced at Stuart, but he cowered in his berth and looked away.

"Stay here," I said. "It's the safest place you can be right now."

I started to inch my way through the main cabin. As I passed Stuart's berth, Stuart looked up at me with wide, fearful eyes.

"What if we sink?" he asked.

"Don't think about it," I answered.

9

With the sailboat pitching and rocking, it was impossible to take a step without grabbing for a handhold and bracing myself. It felt as if we were on a toy boat inside a huge washing machine, being jostled and thrown back and forth.

Crash! Another broadside wave nearly toppled the sailboat. My feet actually left the cabin floor. For a moment I hung by the overhead rail, before swinging back.

Unbelievable . . .

Trying to make my way through the cabin, I was repeatedly slammed in one direction or the other. I finally reached the steps leading up to the companionway door. Suddenly I was aware of a sound I hadn't noticed before. It was a cross between a screaming loud whistle and a roar. A shiver ran through me as I realized it was the wind.

I pressed my shoulder against the companionway door. The sailboat lurched and rocked wildly. It seemed doubtful that it could survive such a beating for long. The companionway door was rattling furiously. The wind outside was screaming. This was a storm the likes of which I'd only read about. Going out there was the last thing in the world any sane person would want to do.

I put my weight against the door and pushed it open. A furious blast of water, spray, and wind hit me. It was like stepping into total soaking mayhem driven at a hundred miles per hour. The wind-driven spray stung, forcing me back into the cabin.

Covering my eyes with one hand and holding on tight with the other, I fought my way out of the cabin and yanked the companionway door closed behind me.

I found the end of the tether attached to my safety harness and tied it to a cockpit rail. Of course, that meant that if the *Big Bucks* went down, I would go with it. Then again, if I got washed overboard in this weather, it wouldn't matter anyway.

Blinding spray and splashing waves were pounding me from all directions, forcing me to cower. I could see the wheel, spinning back and forth wildly every time a wave hit the sailboat.

Another sickening realization hit me. If Mr. Green wasn't at the wheel, then where was he?

I looked up. The green canvas canopy was gone. Ripped clear off the cockpit by the wind, leaving a few bent metal tubes behind.

Wind and spray whipped me from one direction, then another. The way the sailboat was pitching and rocking, it seemed as if the sea were confused, waves coming in all directions at once. I tried to peer outward, but the spray was heavy and blinding. Mixed into it were those long streams of white sea spume, something I had never seen before. At moments there was so much water in the air that it was almost impossible to tell where the sea ended and air began.

Crash! A wave came over the stern and knocked me back against the companionway door with a thud. The cockpit became a bathtub and I was completely immersed. Had I not been wearing the safety harness, I would have been swept away.

"Mr. Green?" I tried to shout, but it felt as if the wind swept the words away almost as soon as they left my lips.

"Mr. Green!" I shouted as loud as I could,

but it was useless. You couldn't hear anything except the screaming roar of the wind.

Crash! Another wave struck. Once again I was momentarily submerged. The sailboat tipped. The danger was getting swept or thrown overboard. Even if the safety harness held, it would be difficult, if not impossible, to get back into the sailboat in these conditions.

Holding the rail tightly, I crawled farther into the cockpit. In a momentary lull as the wind switched directions, I managed to glimpse around. The condition of the cockpit was a total disaster. The radar tower was gone, the flag was gone. I looked up. The Mylar mainsail was a flapping shred flying horizontally from the boom. Broken ropes and wires hung or swayed from the mast. It must have all happened during the knockdown, when a wave the size of a three-story building must have struck the sailboat and washed most of what was above-board away.

So where was Mr. Green?

10

Staying low in the cockpit and keeping my eyes shielded, I looked around again. The driving rain and sea spray made it almost impossible to see. Every few moments the sailboat would rock so far over that it would take every bit of my strength just to hold on and keep from being tossed into the sea.

But where was Mr. Green?

Was he gone? Washed overboard during the knockdown, the tether of his safety harness stretched tight and snapped like a kite string?

And where did that leave the rest of us? Not one of us over the age of fifteen. None of us with any real practical sailing experience, caught in the kind of storm that could easily sink a lifelong sailor with one freak wave. . . .

Get a grip! I told myself. Panicking, worrying about the future—it was all useless. Just stay focused on the next thing. That was all that counted. Just one thing at a time.

Out of the corner of my eye I noticed a thick strand of bright yellow nylon cord jammed tightly against the gunnel of the cockpit and then disappearing over the top. Was it the tether to Mr. Green's safety harness? I stretched to that side of the cockpit and got a handhold.

Just then the sailboat tipped, almost spilling me out of the cockpit. For an instant I felt as if I were hanging by my fingertips from the edge of a cliff. Somehow I managed to hold on, and when the sailboat righted itself, I poked my head out of the cockpit. One moment there were thirty-foot walls of gray-green water surrounding us on all sides as the *Big Bucks* slid down into a wave trough. The next moment she would be lifted up out of the trough and into the howling wind. Then I could see the huge, confused waves churning in every direction. Waves that truly were as big as houses, their tops being sheared off and turned into foam by the violent wind.

I looked again for the yellow cord. It was

stretched tight from the cockpit, across the side deck, and over the edge to the hull. There it disappeared.

But it must have been attached to something heavy, and I had a feeling I knew what that was.

11

I knew I couldn't do it alone. With the wind howling and the sailboat rocking madly, I crawled back down to the companionway door. I pushed it open, heaved myself inside, and shut it behind me.

The cabin was a wreck. Pillows, pots, binoculars, and cushions were strewn everywhere. With the *Big Bucks* still pitching and heaving violently, I dared not stand up. Instead, I crawled through the debris, pushing the junk out of the way and inching my way forward toward the berths.

I reached the chart table and lay there for a moment, curled around the table leg and holding it tightly as I tried to catch my breath. The effort required to hold on was incredibly tiring.

And yet, if we were going to have any chance of surviving, there was still a huge amount of work to do.

After a few moments, when I felt I'd regained some strength, I started again toward the berths.

"Talia?" I called.

"Ian?" She called back from her berth, sounding relieved.

"Stuart?" I called next.

"What's going on?" Stuart cried.

"It's bad," I said, bracing myself against the continual shifts and swings. "I think your dad's hurt. We're gonna have to try to bring him down here."

"What's wrong with him?" Stuart asked.

"I don't know," I said. "I can't see him."

"What do you mean?" Talia asked anxiously.

"I can't explain it," I answered. "When you get out there you'll see."

"You . . . you can't bring him in yourself?" Stuart asked.

"Not a chance," I said, not bothering to add that at that point I didn't know if his father was even alive. "And if we don't get him fast, there may be no point in getting him at all."

"I don't understand," Stuart said, but at the same time he unlatched his bunk board and swung his legs out of his berth. Talia was also getting out. With the sailboat yawing and rolling, and with junk in the cabin shifting and flying everywhere, it took them a long time to pull on life jackets.

When they were ready, we crawled back through the cabin. At the end of the cabin I helped them put on safety harnesses.

"This way, no matter what happens, you can pull yourself back into the cockpit," I explained.

"How bad could it be?" Stuart wondered out loud.

"Just wait," I answered while bracing myself inside the companionway door. "You guys ready?"

Talia nodded slowly. Stuart just stared at me with wide, frightened eyes.

I put my shoulder to the door and pushed. Once again a chaos of wind and water blasted in as soon as the door opened. The howl was louder than ever. I started to crawl out toward the cockpit. With a grim look on her face, Talia followed.

"I don't believe this!" Stuart shouted, shielding his eyes with one hand as he brought up the rear.

A moment later we huddled in the cockpit, holding tight in the wild storm.

"Where's my dad?" Stuart shouted as the

wind and spray raked the loose parts of our rain gear, smacking our faces and making everything whip and flap violently.

I pointed over the side of the cockpit.

"He went over?" Stuart gasped.

"I think so!" I shouted back and gestured to the taut yellow safety harness tether.

"What do we do?" Talia yelled.

"Stuart and I will try to get him!" I shouted back, handing the tether to my safety harness to her. "You feed out our tethers until we get to the side deck, then tie them off so we don't get thrown over the side."

"Gotcha!" Talia shouted back.

I looked at Stuart. I could see the fear in his eyes and I could understand it. You'd have to be crazy not to be scared. I just had to pray that the fear wouldn't paralyze him.

"Ready?" I yelled.

"Okay."

I pulled a snapped jib line out of a cleat. "We need line."

"What for?" Stuart asked.

"Your father," I answered.

In the midst of the mayhem Stuart paused and blinked. "Like the shark?"

"Right." I put the end of the jib line in my mouth. It tasted salty. Then Stuart and I started to climb out of the cockpit.

12

With the sailboat rocking and pitching dangerously, we crawled on our stomachs across the side deck. When we reached the edge where the deck met the hull, I motioned back at Talia to tie our tethers tightly so that no more line played out.

With that done, I put my fingers over the edge of the deck and stretched forward until I could see down into the water. Just as I'd both hoped and feared, Mr. Green hung limply by his harness halfway down the hull.

Each time the sailboat rolled to the leeward side, Stuart's father was dunked in the water. Each time the boat righted itself, Mr. Green would get pulled out, dripping wet, only to be dunked again with the next roll.

"Is he alive?" Stuart cried, looking pale and frightened.

"Only one way to find out!" I yelled back. After testing my tether to make sure it was secure, I reached out over the edge of the deck. It was impossible to reach down the hull to Mr. Green, but when the sailboat rolled and Stuart's father hit the water, he would float up. After a couple of tries, I managed to get the jib line around one of Mr. Green's legs.

I thrust the jib line into Stuart's hands. "On the next roll pull tight and try to tie it off!"

Stuart gripped the jib line tight. Meanwhile, I grabbed the yellow nylon tether line attached to Mr. Green's safety harness.

Once again the *Big Bucks* rolled. Mr. Green's body hit the water and floated up. Stuart and I pulled hard on our lines, then tied them off. Now, when the *Big Bucks* righted itself, Mr. Green hung just below the edge of the deck— almost within reach.

With the sailboat rolling and pitching wildly, it took a Herculean effort to pull Mr. Green up over the edge and onto the side deck. Each time we pulled him up another inch, Stuart and I would secure the rope and tether. It was slow, exhausting, and incredibly scary work. Each effort was followed by a short period where we held on for dear life, taking a rest and trying to gain strength for the next move.

It was a good thing that Stuart was there to help.

Finally we got his father up over the hull and onto the side deck. Mr. Green lay there with his eyes closed, completely drenched and dripping like a big fish.

"Mr. Green!" I shouted at him.

"Dad!" Stuart shouted almost directly in his ear.

There was no response. Stuart gave me a worried look.

I slid my hand inside Mr. Green's soaked rain jacket.

"He feels warm!" I yelled. But in the turbulence it was impossible to feel for a pulse or tell whether Stuart's father was breathing. "We better get him below!"

Given the conditions, it was impossible to handle the man carefully. He was bigger and heavier than any of us. We had to drag him across the side deck, up over the cabin, and into the cockpit. I winced every time Stuart's father banged into a rail or a ledge. In a way you had to feel thankful Mr. Green wouldn't feel it. At least, not until he woke up.

If he woke up.

Meanwhile, Talia, Stuart, and I took some

pretty bad slams ourselves. After one particularly nasty roll I noticed bright red blood running out of my sister's nose. It wasn't a pretty sight, and I hoped it was only bleeding and not broken.

In the cockpit Mr. Green crumpled on the floor like a big broken doll. Talia, Stuart, and I slumped in the cockpit beside him, bracing ourselves and trying to catch our breaths. Talia felt Mr. Green's neck.

"I think I feel a pulse!" she yelled.

"What do you think happened to him?" Stuart asked me.

You could imagine Mr. Green being washed over the side by the huge wave, and unable to climb back into the boat. Meanwhile, each time another wave hurtled against the hull, he must've taken a brutal slamming.

My sister felt around Mr. Green's head. "The right side of his head is really swollen."

Stuart looked at me with an alarmed expression. "What do you think?"

"I think . . . he's lucky to be alive," I answered.

"If we live through this," Stuart yelled, "we'll all be lucky to be alive!"

13

*G*etting Stuart's father belowdecks was another exhausting task. Everyone was incredibly relieved the moment we were all in the main cabin and Stuart was able to bolt the companionway door closed. Inside the cabin we all collapsed in exhaustion while still holding the handholds as the sailboat rolled and bucked.

With each roll Mr. Green groaned and flopped around on the floor like a sack of loose potatoes, but we were too tired to stop him. Short of keeping his head from banging into anything hard, all we could do was watch and hold on.

Meanwhile, the storm showed no sign of letting up. The sailboat was drifting, helpless, like a toy in a bathtub with a little kid thrashing around.

Through a window in the ceiling of the cabin I was watching the grayness of driving rain and sea water when the sailboat suddenly heeled over on its side. Bodies and loose supplies slid across the cabin floor. I waited for the sailboat to right itself, but this time it felt as if it was also sliding sideways down a hill.

Instead of righting itself, the *Big Bucks* began to tip over more.

Talia screamed.

Stuart yelped.

For a split second through the overhead cabin window I saw nothing but dark green. Then we all went flying.

14

I was vaguely aware of being flung from one side of the cabin to the other, and then thrown completely upside down and hitting the ceiling. A split second later I was dumped in a tangle of bodies and debris on the cabin floor. The *Big Bucks* had literally rolled over 360 degrees. Bodies, debris, supplies, and even pieces of furniture had fallen on me.

Everything inside the cabin had been bathed in cold water.

Now I lay in that rocking mess. With each sway of the sailboat, a big can of Hawaiian Punch on the floor rolled toward me. It stopped with its smiley face grinning at me, then rolled away.

So many parts of my body hurt that I didn't

know where to start counting. But the most throbbing, stinging pain was coming from the last two fingers of my left hand. I would have tried to feel them with my right hand, but my right arm was trapped under someone's body.

"Anyone okay?" I asked wearily.

Over the howl and the banging and thrashing I could hear my sister sobbing.

"Talia?" I said.

"I'm . . . I'm hurt," she sobbed, "but I think I'm okay."

"Stuart?" I said.

"My head," Stuart groaned.

"What's going on?" Mr. Green suddenly asked groggily.

I was surprised. The jolt that had nearly knocked out the rest of us must have woken him up.

"You're in the cabin," I answered.

"Uhhhh . . ." Mr. Green moaned.

"Are you okay?" I asked.

Stuart's father didn't answer. I had a feeling he'd slipped into unconsciousness again.

Outside, the violent rocking and jarring continued nonstop. Only now every lurching move by the sailboat resulted in a stab of pain. Talia was still sobbing. What if she was hurt worse than she thought?

Despite the pain and fatigue I felt, I knew I

had to do something. We couldn't all just lay there in a heap on the floor until the next big wave flung us around like loose beans inside a jar. The first thing I had to do was gather my own limbs from under the others.

I slowly eased myself out of the tangle of limbs, furniture, and supplies. By now I knew that the ring finger and pinkie of my left hand had to be broken, based on the pain I felt and the odd angles at which they were bent back and wouldn't come forward.

"Talia?" I said. "How're you doing?"

My sister raised her head. Her beautiful blond hair was a wet tangle. Her nose and mouth were smeared with blood. Her eyes were red and streaked with tears. "I don't know. My right side really hurts."

"Try to feel it," I urged her. "See if anything's broken."

Meanwhile, Stuart had also managed to free himself from the pile. Blood dripped down his face from a nasty-looking gash over his eyebrow, and he had a big bruise on his cheek. He wiped some blood away with his hand and stared at his reddened fingers in horror.

"Am I okay?" he gasped fearfully.

"Sometimes head wounds bleed a lot," Talia said. "Put pressure on it."

Stuart scooped up a sweatshirt from the

cabin floor and pressed it against his forehead. "Now what?" he asked.

The words were hardly out of his mouth when the sailboat rolled again, and we all tumbled from one side of the cabin to the other.

"I can't take this," Talia sobbed.

"What's going on?" Mr. Green asked groggily. Once again the jostling seemed to wake him momentarily.

"Dad?" Stuart said hopefully.

There was no reply. Mr. Green was gone again.

"We have to get him into a berth," Talia said. "We can't let him roll around like this."

Slowly and painfully, despite the constant crashing, we managed to get Mr. Green into one of the cabin berths and close the bunk board. Short of another total rollover, he would be safe.

Now we could all see the side of Mr. Green's head. It was swollen and discolored. He must've taken one heck of a nasty blow.

The rest of us climbed back into our berths. I was soaking wet, cold, in pain, and as miserable as I could ever remember. Not to mention thoroughly exhausted. And while I doubted any of us would be able to sleep during this storm, I thought if I could just put my head down, I'd feel better.

We spent the rest of the day in our berths. The banging and flailing didn't let up, but being thrown around in our berths, we couldn't go far. I lost count of the number of times the sailboat was flung over on one side or the other. But thankfully there were no more 360-degree rolls.

Then, at some point finally, the rocking seemed to gradually diminish. I couldn't tell exactly when, because by then I was asleep.

15

I slept in fits and starts, often waking in pain, finding a slightly more comfortable position, and quickly falling back to sleep. When my eyes finally did open, sunlight was pouring in through the overhead cabin window, and the sailboat seemed still. I lay in my berth for several moments, staring up in disbelief at the blue sky through the window above. All I could hear was the breathing of the others and the mild slosh of the sea against the boat's hull.

The fingers on my left hand throbbed painfully, and a dozen different spots on my body ached—especially my elbows and knees. But another sensation was making itself known—hunger. I hadn't eaten a thing the entire previous day. For me that was almost as miraculous as surviving the storm.

With my right hand I lowered the bunk board and stiffly swung my legs out of the berth. My clothes were warm and wet. In the other berths the Greens were still asleep, but Talia's berth was empty. Around me the cabin was an incredible wreck. Even though the refrigerator and lockers had latches, nearly every one of them had opened and spilled its contents. The blanket of debris, cans, cushions, tools, and whatever on the floor was several inches thick. Even though I was starving after nearly forty-eight hours without food, the combined smells of spilled relish, mustard, and vanilla left me slightly nauseated.

Feeling an intense desire to get out in the open air, and curious to see where my sister was, I stepped carefully through the wet debris on the cabin floor and paused by the chart table. In the wall beside the chart table was the radio. I flicked it on, but nothing happened. I tried a light. That was dead, too. It didn't make sense. We'd had electricity during the storm, but now it was gone. Why?

It was something I'd have to figure out later. Right now I just wanted to get outside. I climbed up the companionway steps. After that storm, coming out of the cabin and feeling the warm, sun-lit air was almost as big a shock as the impact of that first huge wave that had knocked the sailboat down. Only this was a pleasant shock that passed quickly.

Abovedecks the *Big Bucks* was a total disaster. The tall aluminum mast had snapped. With the exception of the stainless-steel railing, everything else had broken off and washed away. I found Talia sitting up at the bow with her back to me.

"You okay?" I came up behind her.

"Don't look, Ian," she warned me softly with a sniff.

"Hey, I'm your brother," I said, putting my hand on her shoulder.

"It's all my fault." Talia sniffed. "If I hadn't made you come on this stupid trip—"

"You didn't *make* me come," I said. "I wouldn't have come if I didn't want to. Now let me see. I have to make sure you're okay."

Talia allowed me to turn her shoulders. When I saw my sister's face, I felt an involuntary grimace. Her eyes were blackened and her nose was swollen to twice it's normal size.

I forced a smile. "Nice."

"Don't, Ian," Talia said wearily. "It's not funny."

"Hey, we're alive, aren't we?" I said. "Look

at the boat. She got pretty beat up, too. What about your side? Last night you said it hurt."

"It's sore, but I think it's okay," Talia said. "I just banged into so many things. What about you?"

"Totally banged up, but basically okay except for this." I held up my left hand.

"Oh, Ian!" Talia gasped when she saw my ring and pinkie fingers sticking up at strange angles. "Does it hurt?"

"Only when I hit it with a hammer." I grinned.

"It looks horrible," Talia said. "What about Stuart and his father?"

"I think they're both still sleeping," I said.

"Shouldn't we wake them up?" Talia asked.

"Why?" I asked.

"To do something," Talia said. "Like call for help."

I shook my head slowly. "There's nothing to call with. The antennas are gone, the radio's dead. A boat like this is supposed to have an EPIRB."

"A what?" Talia asked.

"Emergency Position Indicating Radio-beacon," I explained. "It's battery-powered and sends out an SOS signal. It's supposed to go on automatically if we roll over."

"Which we definitely did yesterday," Talia said.

"Right," I said. "Not that there's any guarantee anyone will pick up the signal. The other thing we have to do is to watch for a ship and fire a flare when we see one."

"You think we'll see one?" Talia asked.

"Sooner or later," I answered. "It's not like we're way out in the ocean. There's a lot of boat traffic on the Gulf."

"There you are." Behind us, Stuart came up on deck. Talia quickly turned away, although I couldn't understand why she cared what he thought.

Stuart himself wasn't looking so hot. He was limping, and the bruise on his cheek had turned an angry bluish-purple color. He was still holding the sweatshirt against the gash over his eyebrow.

"When I woke up and you weren't there, I thought maybe you'd split," he said.

"Where would we go?" I asked.

"I don't know," Stuart answered. "Maybe you decided to swim the rest of the way. What a wreck, huh?"

Now Talia turned and looked at him.

"Wow." Stuart grinned. "You look worse than me."

"Thanks," Talia said sarcastically. "How's that cut?"

"I don't know," Stuart answered. "I can't get the sweatshirt off. It feels like it's glued on."

"I know what to do," Talia said. She got up and went back down into the cabin.

Meanwhile, I noticed that Stuart was carrying a red plastic box the size and shape of a briefcase. Inside were the emergency flares.

"How's your dad?" I asked.

"Not so good," Stuart answered. "He wakes up but doesn't act like he's all there. Then he goes out again."

"He must've gotten hit on the head pretty hard," I said.

"I just think we better get help fast." With his free hand Stuart started to open the flare kit.

"You sure you want to use those?" I asked.

"Sure," Stuart said. "Why not?"

"Because if we can't see a ship, what makes you think anyone's close enough to see our flare?" I asked.

Stuart frowned. "I thought that was the whole point. You shoot the flares so that they'll see you."

I shook my head. "You shoot the flares when *you* see *them*. The idea is to get their attention. You can shoot those flares now if you want, but if there's no one close enough to see, you'll be wasting them."

Stuart opened the flare kit. He started to read the instructions inside.

"Suppose you shoot those flares now and no one sees them," I said. "And then suppose sometime tonight we see the lights of a ship way off in the distance. How are you going to get their attention if all your flares are gone?"

Stuart made a face. "So you're saying we just sit here and wait?"

"For now," I said.

"And what about my father?" Stuart asked.

Just then Talia came back up from below. She looked grim. "I think we have a problem."

With Talia in the lead, we climbed down the companionway steps into the main cabin. I thought I heard a slight splash. Ahead of me, Stuart stopped. The floor of the main cabin was covered by about an inch of water, although you could barely see it with all the junk on the floor.

"What is it?" I asked.

"Water," Stuart answered. "What's it doing in here?"

I could think of only one answer. The hull had been damaged in the storm. The *Big Bucks* was sinking.

16

Stuart turned white when I delivered the news.

"What do we do?" he gasped.

"We should get your dad above and find the life raft," I said. "Then we should probably try to keep the *Big Bucks* afloat as long as possible."

"Why?" Stuart asked.

"Because if you think we're hard to see now," I said, "just wait until we're in a raft."

"You can't do anything until we fix your hand," Talia said.

Still holding the sweatshirt against his eyebrow, Stuart winced when he saw my bent fingers. "Gee, doesn't that hurt?"

"Better believe it," I answered and turned to

my sister. I was trying not to think of my hand, but the throbbing pain was a constant reminder. "What can you do?"

Talia pursed her lips thoughtfully. "I know what you're supposed to do, but I don't think you're going to like it. You're supposed to bend the fingers back and then tape them to the next healthy finger so they can't move."

At the thought of it an involuntary groan rose into my throat. But the *Big Bucks* was sinking, and whatever had to be done had to be done now.

"I guess we better go find some tape or a first-aid kit or something," I said.

"I want to check on my dad again." Stuart moved toward Mr. Green's berth in the front of the main cabin.

Talia and I started to search through the debris on the floor for a first-aid kit. Talia found one under a cushion.

"Here we go," she said, opening it. "Hey, lucky you. Not only is there tape, but these finger splints." She held up two flat wooden splints that looked like overgrown Popsicle sticks.

I held out my hand and closed my eyes. "Just do it fast and get it over with."

Talia took hold of my fingers and wrenched them back into position. The bolt of blinding hot pain made me scream. I must've jumped five feet.

"What was that?" It was Stuart, looking up from his father's berth at the other end of the cabin.

"N-nothing," I gasped. My entire body trembled from the jolt of pain. I staggered back toward my sister and held out my hand. The fingers were now pointing in the correct direction.

"Sorry," Talia said softly as she taped each finger to a flat wooden split. "Does this hurt?"

"Piece of cake compared to what I just went through." I groaned.

After she finished splinting each finger, Talia taped both of them to my next healthy finger. She cut the tape with a small scissors that had come in the first-aid kit. "There, that's about the best I can do."

"Thanks." We both turned toward Stuart, who was still looking down at his father.

"How's he doing?" I asked.

"Not good," Stuart answered. "I mean, he's breathing, but he still won't wake up."

"Let me fix your head, Stuart," Talia said, going toward him with the scissors.

"Whoa!" Stuart held up his hands to stop her. "I'm not sure I'm ready for surgery."

"All I'm going to do is cut away the

sweatshirt so you don't have to keep holding it," Talia explained.

"Oh." Stuart gave her that goofy grin. "Good idea. I'm not gonna be much help moving my father as long as I have to hold this against my head."

"I'll help you move him," I volunteered. I took a step, but Talia blocked my path.

"You're not going to be able to do much with that hand," she said. "Why don't you let me help Stuart move him?"

"Okay."

Talia went to work cutting away the sweatshirt. Meanwhile, I looked around for a manual bilge pump. A boat like the *Big Bucks* had electric bilge pumps galore, but with the electrical system out, they were useless. And now I knew why the electrical system was down. The leaking sea water had no doubt flooded the battery compartments.

I kept looking for the manual pumps. I didn't know if we could keep a boat the size of the *Big Bucks* afloat with manual pumps, but it was worth a try.

I found two of them. Both came with hoses as wide as those found on vacuum cleaners. But neither hose was long enough to stretch out the companionway door and over the side of the hull. Someone wasn't thinking when they'd put these pumps on board. But they might still work. I went through the toolbox and found a screwdriver.

I was busy unscrewing one of the cabin windows when Stuart and Talia came past with Mr. Green. Over Stuart's eyebrow was a piece of green sweatshirt about the size of a baseball. At its center it turned dark brown with dried blood.

Stuart and Talia were on either side of Mr. Green, holding him up. Mr. Green was still out of it, but the good news was that with help he could put one foot in front of the other and do something that resembled walking.

"Is he any better?" I asked.

Talia shook her head.

"What are you doing?" Stuart asked me.

I explained that I was taking the window off so that we could get a bilge hose outside. "After you get your dad outside, you could come back and help me."

Stuart stared disdainfully at the small manual bilge pumps. "You really think these'll work?"

"No, but it's worth a try," I replied.

Stuart and Talia helped Mr. Green through the cabin and out to the cockpit. By the time Stuart came back, the water level on the cabin floor had risen to my ankles. The *Big Bucks* was still sinking, and that scared me more than the storm the day before.

"You want to grab that pump and get to work?" I said.

Stuart hesitated. "Is that an order?"

"No, it's a request," I replied. "Unless you'd prefer sinking."

Stuart picked up the other plastic pump and started working it by hand. Talia came down into the cabin.

"What should I do?" she asked.

"You better find the raft," I said. "It's probably stowed in the forward cabin."

Talia went into the forward cabin to look. I kept pumping. With a slurping noise, the water from the floor was sucked up through the pump and out the hose in the window, splashing into the sea. Meanwhile, the sun was rising outside. The air in the main cabin was still and hot. Stuart and I were starting to sweat.

"I don't understand why we're doing this." Stuart paused to wipe the sweat off his forehead. "If the boat's gonna sink, shouldn't we let it? We're just wasting energy and sweat trying to keep it afloat. We'll dehydrate ourselves. Why don't we just get into the raft?"

"Two reasons," I answered without stopping. "The first is, right now, we don't *have* a raft. And even when we find it, we don't know that it'll work properly. Believe me, you won't want to see this boat go down if all we have is an uninflated raft. The second reason is exposure. Once we're in that raft, we'll be cooking in the sun. That's when you'll see what dehydration is really like."

"You act like you know a lot," Stuart grumbled as he started to pump again. "Where did you learn so much? Playing with toy boats in the bathtub?"

It was a nasty remark, but there was some truth to it. Much of what I knew, or *thought* I knew, came from stories I'd read in sailing magazines, and in paperbacks like *Adrift*. My actual experience in this stuff was almost zero.

"Found it!" Talia called from the forward cabin. "But it's too heavy!"

"You'd better help her," I said to Stuart.

"Aye, aye, Captain." Stuart's words were filled with sarcasm. He dropped the plastic pump and splashed toward the forward cabin. Through the cabin door I could see Talia struggling with a white rectangular canister the size and shape of a very large suitcase. I felt relieved when I saw it. The raft inside was going to be large enough for all four of us.

"Push it out through the hatch," I called as I pumped.

Stuart reached up and pushed open the forward cabin hatch. He and Talia shoved the canister up on the deck. Then they came through the cabin and went above decks. I remained below and kept pumping. By now the sea water was several inches above my ankles.

We were loosing the battle to keep the *Big Bucks* afloat.

"Ian?" Talia stuck her head into the cabin. She looked serious and pale. "You'd better come up here."

"Something wrong with the raft?" I asked.

"No, something else."

I reluctantly dropped the pump and climbed up abovedecks. If the problem wasn't the raft, then I assumed it was with Mr. Green. Out in the bright sun I had to shield my eyes. But Mr. Green was lying in a shaded part of the cockpit. His face had color and he appeared to be breathing. I looked around. The raft was still in its canister. Both Stuart and Talia had stopped what they were doing and were staring at the water.

At first, in the glare of the sun, I didn't see anything. Then I saw long dark torpedo shapes gliding under the water. A gray dorsal fin cut through the surface.

Sharks. . . .

17

"Now what?" Stuart asked, his voice high and nervous again.

"We'd better keep pumping," I said. I turned to Talia. "And we have to load up on water. I hope someone's out looking for us. But just in case they're not, we have to have enough water to survive. Look for cans, jars, anything you can fill with water, then load up from the faucet in the galley."

I headed back down to the main cabin, and Talia followed. By now the water was nearly up to our knees. Spare life preservers, cushions, cans of food, and plastic bags floated around in the cabin. The red and white first-aid kit floated by, and I grabbed it. Talia started searching for water canisters. I found a pump and went back to work. I had no idea how long the *Big Bucks* would stay afloat. But the longer, the better.

I heard footsteps as Stuart came down into the cabin. "Shouldn't we get the raft inflated?" he asked.

"It won't take long," I answered as I labored over the pump. "But we have to stay on this boat as long as we can."

I hoped Stuart would pick up the other pump, but the guy just stood there with his hands on his hips.

"I know why those sharks came," he said. "I once did a report on them for school. They felt the splashing from these pumps. It sounded like a fish in distress."

"So?" I said as I pumped.

"So if you didn't start using these pumps, they wouldn't have come," Stuart said accusingly.

I kept pumping. "If I didn't pump we'd sink."

"We could use the raft," Stuart countered.

"You really want to get in the raft now that those sharks are around?" I asked. "I already told you we'll be harder to see in a raft. And a lot of things can go wrong."

"Like what?" Stuart asked.

"Like they've been known to deflate," I said as I pumped. "They've been known to spring leaks. Or we could get into it and tomorrow another storm might blow in. If you think it was bad in *this* boat during a storm, just wait until you're in a raft during one."

"How do you know so much?" Stuart asked with a sneer.

"Because I've read about it, okay?" I said, breathing hard as I worked. "In the 1979 Fasnet Race—that's an open ocean race in the British Isles—a storm blew up and a lot of sailors abandoned their boats for their life rafts. All kinds of things went wrong. More than a dozen people died. A lot of them died just trying to jump from their sailboats to their life rafts. Now why don't you pick up the other pump and keep pumping?"

"Why don't you drop dead!" Stuart shot back and climbed back out.

Talia and I shared a long look. Then I turned back to the hand bilge pump. It was clearly a losing battle. The water was slowly rising over my knees. But I had to keep trying. Meanwhile, Talia found some jars and took them over to the galley sink.

"Ian?" I heard her say a little while later.

I looked up. "Yeah?"

"The faucet doesn't work."

I sloshed across the main cabin and into the galley. I tried the faucets, but not a drop of water came out. I opened the cabinet under the sink and stared inside. All I saw was thin metal tubing, some of it under water. I muttered a curse under my breath.

"What should we do?" Talia asked.

"We have to find water," I said. "Otherwise we could be in really big trouble."

18

"What's going on?" A little while later Stuart stuck his head through the companionway and into the main cabin. It seemed like he'd calmed down.

I explained that despite the fact that there had to be a large water tank somewhere in the bowels of the *Big Bucks,* we couldn't get any water.

"You don't think someone'll find us before not having water becomes a problem?" Stuart asked.

"I don't know if we'll be found or not," I answered. "What I do know is that we're going to have to get into the raft soon. And if we're out there more than a day, it'll get mighty unpleasant without water."

"We've got this." Talia reached into the water filling the main cabin and picked up the large can of Hawaiian Punch.

"Try to find everything you can that's drinkable," I urged her and continued pumping.

"Why don't you give that up already?" Stuart asked.

"If we were both pumping instead of arguing, maybe we'd be able to keep this sailboat afloat," I answered. "Then we wouldn't have to worry about the raft."

"We should've shot those flares," Stuart grumbled as he turned and went back abovedecks. "We probably would've been rescued by now."

I shook my head wearily. I may have only been twelve and a half, but that was old enough to know that *should've, would've,* and *could've* weren't going to keep us alive. I turned to Talia. "Keep looking for stuff to eat and drink. I'll keep pumping."

But by now the water had risen to mid-thigh. Stuart was right about one thing—we weren't going to keep this sailboat afloat much longer. But the alternative, being stuck in that raft, made me pump twice as hard.

Meanwhile, Talia kept sloshing around, looking for water and food. That meant the two of us were down below, leaving Stuart and his father with the raft on the deck above. As I pumped, I had to fight off the nagging image of Stuart pulling his father into the raft and stealing away, leaving Talia and me to go down with the ship.

"Hey, look." Talia held up a large, water-filled plastic gallon jug marked in blue letters EMERGENCY DRINKING WATER.

"Great," I said. "That's a start."

"It's the end, too," Talia said. "I've searched high and low."

In that heat a gallon of water and a can of Hawaiian Punch wouldn't last the four of us long. I hoped there was more to drink somewhere on board. By now the level of the water in the cabin had risen almost to my waist. I was losing the battle to keep the *Big Bucks* afloat. Maybe it was time to give up and look for water instead.

Suddenly I heard a sizzling sound from abovedecks. I thought I knew what it was. I grabbed an overhead rail and hauled myself out of the flood belowdecks.

Just as I feared, Stuart was standing on the cabin top, holding one of our three flares above his head, looking like the Statue of Liberty. The flare hissed and glowed as it burned, but in the daylight it was barely noticeable.

I managed to keep myself from pointing out

Stuart's stupidity. It wasn't easy. Instead I picked up the package with the two remaining flares inside and stuck it inside my life vest.

"Gave up pumping, huh?" Stuart taunted me. "Lot of good it did us. All it did was bring the sharks around."

I looked at the water. The dark torpedo shapes were still skimming around us, just a few feet beneath the surface. Now and then a dorsal fin would cut the water.

"So, now what?" Stuart asked.

I tried to think it all through. We had a minimal amount of water, some food, flares, flashlights, a first-aid kit. In a worst case scenario, what else would we need?

"Got any fishing tackle?" I asked.

Stuart grinned at me like I'd gone mad. "What for? Gonna do some fishing while we pass the time?"

"It's just in case we run out of food," I tried to explain.

"And suppose we catch a fish?" Stuart said. "What are we gonna cook it with?"

"We're not," I replied.

"Oh, we're gonna eat it raw?" Stuart grinned. "A little sushi?"

"Don't be a jerk, Stuart," Talia snapped. "Ian's only trying to help."

"Oh, sure," Stuart practically spit. "He's done

a great job so far. Refusing to use the flares to bring help and insisting on pumping out a sinking boat, which only brought the sharks."

I didn't have the time or energy to argue. I turned to my sister. "Don't go anywhere," I said, and then went back down into the cabin to see if I could find some fishing tackle.

Belowdecks, the water was up to my chest. I waded into it nervously. The boat would go down soon. What would happen if it went down with me inside it?

In my memory of all the junk that had fallen out of the lockers during the storm, I couldn't recall seeing any fishing tackle. I quickly started going through the few lockers that had remained closed. Sure enough, in one I found a dropline with some hooks.

I quickly waded back through the cabin and climbed up the companionway. By now the *Big Bucks* was so low in the water that the sea had practically reached her decks.

"Looks like we'd better get into the raft," I said. "Come on, Stuart, give me a hand." I went around to one side of the raft canister and started to tie a rope from the raft to the sail-boat's railing. At the same time I waited for Stuart to pick up the other side.

Stuart just stood there with his hands on his hips. "What do you want me to do?"

"We have to throw this thing overboard," I explained. "When it hits the water, the raft is supposed to inflate automatically."

"Wait," Stuart said. "Why don't we inflate it here and all get into it first? Then we can just wait for the sailboat to sink out from under us."

"You don't know what she's gonna do when she sinks," I answered. "If the stern goes first, it could tip the bow up. The raft could get caught in the rail or on a halyard and take us straight down with it."

To my surprise, Stuart didn't argue. He and I slid the canister off the cabin. It hit the water with a splash and immediately split open. With a loud hiss the orange-and-black raft inside began to inflate automatically.

The raft was the shape of an octagon, like a stop sign. The flotation walls were two thick black tubes, one on top of the other, like a backyard kiddy pool's, only thicker. Rising above the tubes was an orange tent-shaped canopy to protect us from the sun and waves. It looked to me like a six-man raft, capable of keeping six people afloat.

Up till that point, the sharks had been cruising steadily around the sailboat. But the vibration of the raft striking the water seemed to ignite them. They suddenly broke formation and darted toward the raft, passing close beside or under it as if checking to see if it was something edible. One of them even butted the raft with his snout, as if double-checking just to make sure.

Standing on the cabin, Talia, Stuart and I shared a nervous look. None of us was looking forward to being in the water with those beasts.

19

The next job would be getting Stuart's father into the raft. We pulled in the tether until the raft floated beside the sailboat. Moving a semi-conscious two-hundred-pound man across a deck and into a small raft was no easy job. Stuart grabbed his father by the shoulders. I lifted Mr. Green's legs. We slid him slowly toward the raft. By now the outside water level was almost up to the deck. The good news was that it would make it easier to slide Mr. Green off the sailboat deck and into the raft.

Stuart stepped to the edge of the deck and started to pull his father toward the opening in the raft's canopy. Talia also leaned at the deck's edge, trying to hold the raft steady. I suspected that in the back of our minds we were all thinking the same thing—if Mr. Green slipped out of our hands and went into the water, the sharks would get him in no time.

"Easy," I cautioned, although it was probably unnecessary. By now Stuart was leaning off the deck, trying to angle his father's head and shoulders through the opening in the canopy.

Suddenly the *Big Bucks* shifted under us, heeling slightly toward the raft. Talia and I dived for the railing to keep from falling into the water. Over my shoulder I saw Stuart let go of his father and balance on one leg, swinging his arms wildly as if to throw his weight toward the sailboat's deck.

"Ahhhhh!" Stuart screamed in terror as his momentum threw him into the sea with a *splash!*

20

The *Big Bucks,* now almost completely awash, slowly righted itself. I took in the scene all at once. Stuart was screaming and thrashing wildly in the water beside the boat. The dark torpedo shapes under the surface were rocketing in toward him. The raft was floating away from the sailboat. Luckily, the same force that threw Stuart overboard had dumped Mr. Green into the life raft, where he now lay in an almost comical position with his feet coming out of the canopy and aiming toward the sky.

"Help!" Stuart cried. Almost simultaneously Talia and I dived to the edge of the deck, grabbed Stuart's flailing arms, and yanked him out of the water.

Snap! As if sensing it was about to lose

lunch, a shark lunged out of the water and tried to take a bite, missing Stuart's legs by inches.

Talia, Stuart, and I tumbled back onto the deck. *Thunk!* I felt a sharp jolt of pain as my back hit a corner of the cockpit. Out of the corner of my eye I saw the raft stretch to the end of its tether and then stop.

Seeing that everyone was safe and we still had the raft, I closed my eyes and breathed a deep sigh of relief. That was close. The pain in my back throbbed, and now my elbow began to sting. I suspected that I'd scraped it pretty hard while trying to save Stuart.

But at least we were okay.

21

"**Y**ou tried to get me killed!"

I opened my eyes. Dripping seawater, Stuart stood over me with his hands in fists.

"What?" I asked in disbelief.

"Don't pretend you don't know." Stuart shook his fist at me.

"You're crazy! We pulled you out!" I yelled in frustration and jumped to my feet.

"Sure. You chickened out!" Stuart yelled back.

Something in me snapped. Stuart might have been older and bigger than me. Maybe even stronger. But it didn't matter. Balling my good hand into a fist and my bad hand into something resembling half a fist, I charged him.

Stuart's mouth fell open and his hands went toward his face.

"Don't, Ian!" Talia cried.

I stopped and glared into Stuart's eyes searchingly. Was he ready to fight?

Stuart averted his eyes.

I felt the rage seep out of me. What good would fighting do? I unclenched my fists and shook my head. Beneath our feet the *Big Bucks* was now almost completely swamped.

"We'd better get everything we can into the raft," Talia said.

Even though the *Big Bucks* was close to sinking, I ducked through the companionway and back into the main cabin. By now the level of the water was up to my collarbone, but in a strange way it was cooling and soothing after my run-in with that idiot Stuart. Cans and water-tight packages floated inside the cabin and I grabbed as many as I could and handed them back to Talia in the cockpit.

I had to hope that we would be rescued soon.

Maybe even within the hour.

But the truth was, you never knew.

It might take days.

Or even longer.

So I took everything I could. By now the water level was up to my chin, and it was time to leave the main cabin for good. I actually had to duck under the water and swim out through the companionway. We would not be going back in.

We got all the supplies into the raft and then managed to climb in without any repeats of the near-disaster with Stuart. The sharks did come back, however. It seemed as if every unusual movement or splash peaked their interest.

Even though it was a six-man raft and there were only four of us, it felt cramped with bodies and supplies. At first we all slid toward the center, along with cans of food, flashlights, and other supplies. The floor was made of heavy, rubberized canvas. It was strong, but not very supportive, and we all sank into the middle as if we were sitting in a hammock.

Talia, Stuart, and I managed to sit up. Around our heads heavy nylon straps hung from the ceiling of the canopy. Mr. Green lay in the middle of the floor, unconscious, but breathing steadily.

"What are these things?" Talia asked, tugging at one of the nylon straps hanging around our faces.

"I'm not sure," I answered. "Maybe to hold on to when things get rough."

"This is crazy." Stuart contributed his usual unhelpful remarks as we twisted and squirmed in a futile attempt to find comfortable positions. The heavy smell of plastic, rubber, and talc from the newly opened raft didn't help.

"We need to stow everything," I said. "It'll help create a counterbalance."

The interior of the raft was lined with netting. We slowly began to stow our supplies. Meanwhile, in the netting I found additional supplies, including another EPIRB, which appeared to have gone on automatically when the raft inflated. There was also a first-aid kit, as well as more flares, eight pint-size cans of emergency water, a hand pump, and a flashlight.

"Hey, cool," Stuart said as he opened the raft's flare kit. Inside was a small red plastic pistol and six small flares about the size of shotgun shells. Stuart read the print on them. " 'Meteor flares.' Each one of these things is supposed to go two hundred feet in the air and stay lit for thirty seconds."

"There isn't room for everything," Talia said, gesturing at the cans and water-tight bags still heaped in the middle of the raft around Mr. Green. "What about all the rest of this stuff?"

"Let's take care of Stuart's dad first and worry about the rest later," I said.

"What do you mean?" Stuart asked.

"We can't just leave him lying in the middle of the raft," I explained. "We'll have to—"

I never got to finish the sentence. Suddenly the raft tipped up on one side and began to thrash back and forth wildly. Inside, Stuart, Talia and I were all thrown around like dolls in a sack. The cans of provisions and supplies still on the raft floor clanked and banged together. Mr. Green's arms and legs flopped around, banging into everyone.

"What's going on!?" Stuart cried.

I grabbed one of the straps hanging from the canopy to keep from being tossed around. I had no idea what was happening.

22

The shaking stopped almost as suddenly as it had started. I cautiously looked out of the canopy opening and down into the green-blue water just in time to see a long dark shadow swim lazily out from under the raft.

"Shark," I muttered.

"It must've been huge!" Stuart gasped.

"Twelve feet at least," I replied. My heart was pounding hard. The darn thing had been as thick as a horse. Had it bitten one of the inflated tubes? I listened carefully, but all I heard was the mild dipping and sloshing of the raft in the water. Next I pressed my fingers against the insides of the raft walls.

"What are you doing?" Talia asked.

"Making sure we're not losing air," I said.

"Oh, please, no!" Stuart whimpered.

The two tubes that made up the raft wall felt solid. I felt relieved.

"Maybe it just banged us around with its tail," Talia guessed.

"Who knows?" Still shaking, I looked back at Stuart's father, who was now lying facedown on the raft's floor with his arms going out at odd angles. "Like I was saying, we have to secure your father so that he doesn't flop around."

"You mean, for the next time a shark attacks?" Stuart asked.

"Or if the wind and waves kick up," I said, looking around the raft. Folded into the mesh was something silvery. I pulled it out. Good, a space blanket.

With the space blanket, we were able to make a man-sized sling that would basically keep Mr. Green lashed to one corner of the raft. The blanket was made of a silvery material designed to keep heat in. It would help keep Mr. Green warm. When Talia, Stuart, and I each sat in the other three corners, the raft became steady and the bottom began to flatten out.

The next problem was the supplies still left in the middle of the floor.

"Why don't we just dump this stuff?" Stuart

asked. "We're bound to be rescued before we need it."

"Says who?" I replied.

"You hear about it all the time on the news," Stuart said. "People stranded in the Gulf being rescued by the Coast Guard."

"Sure," I replied. "If a fishing boat goes out in the morning and doesn't come back at night, someone's going to figure out that something's wrong. But we're not supposed to reach Mexico for at least four more days. My mom doesn't expect to hear from us till then. Does anyone expect to hear from you?"

"Not really," Stuart said.

"Not only that," Talia added, "but if Mom doesn't hear from us for a couple of days after we're supposed to get to Mexico, she'll probably figure we're just having a good time and forgot to call."

"What we have to do is get as much junk as we can out of the raft," I said.

"Throw it out?" Talia asked uncertainly.

"No, tie it to the outside of the raft." I began to wriggle.

"What are you doing?" Stuart asked caustically.

"I'm taking my pants off," I informed him.

"Have you lost your mind?" Stuart asked.

"You'll see," I said.

"I don't want to see," Stuart shot back.

"Don't be stupid," I grunted. I was wearing a bathing suit underneath. Once I had my pants off, I knotted the bottom of each leg tightly. Then I packed the legs with cans of food, the big can of Hawaiian Punch, and other supplies. Finally I pulled my belt tightly through the belt loops, closing off the waist as if it was the opening of a sack. After tying a line around the belt, I heaved the bulky pants into the water. It quickly sank a few feet down. Then the line went tight. Finally the floor of the raft was clear.

"Aw, my hero," Stuart said in a fake, high-pitched voice.

I ignored him and stared out the opening of the canopy. A dozen yards away the seawater lapped over the decks of the *Big Bucks* and splashed lightly against the cabin. Talia, Stuart, and I watched in silence as the stern slowly slid under. The *Big Bucks*'s bow rose a few feet out of the water and hung for a moment. Then the sailboat slid backward and disappeared beneath the surface, leaving a momentary boil of air bubbles and a few swirls before disappearing forever.

23

The minutes passed slowly in our cramped quarters. The thin bottom of the raft gave each time one of us shifted positions. You couldn't move without disturbing someone else. To make things worse, Mr. Green jerked and groaned in his semiconscious state, sometimes shifting his weight and making everyone grab for the straps hanging from the canopy.

Every time I moved, something hurt. My skin rubbed painfully against the rubber walls and raft bottom. It felt as if there wasn't a spot on my body that wasn't scraped, red, or sore. And I had to assume Talia and Stuart felt the same way.

I gazed out the canopy opening. The sun was high above us. Sunlight glared off the water and into my eyes. I scanned the horizon for a sign of a ship, but the dark shadows of the circling sharks constantly distracted me.

It seemed as if they were just biding their time, waiting.

Meanwhile, the canopy protected us from the direct rays of sun, but under the canopy, it was sweltering.

"Wouldn't mind a little breeze," Stuart mumbled.

I wouldn't have minded a breeze, either, but I knew we would mind the waves that would inevitably come with it.

"How about something to drink?" Stuart asked.

I reached for the emergency water jug.

"What are we going to drink out of?" Talia asked.

I looked around, but couldn't find anything.

Stuart grinned. "Hey, looks like Mr. Perfect forgot to bring something to drink out of."

Stuart's barbs irritated me. "Why didn't *you* think of bringing something to drink out of?" I snapped back.

"I guess I just assumed you had everything under control," Stuart answered with a smirk. "Well, we can always use our hands."

"No," I said.

"Why not, Mr. Survival Expert?" Stuart taunted.

Once again it was hard for me to resist hauling back and belting Stuart, but I managed. "Because we'll waste too much. We don't know how long we're going to be in this raft, so we have to conserve water."

"Oh, yeah? Well, guess what?" Stuart asked as he reached for the water jug. "It's not even *your* water. It's *my* water because it was on *my* boat. So I'll take as much as I want."

"Don't be a jerk, Stuart," Talia snapped, then turned to me. "We can take apart one of the flashlights and drink the water out of the plastic part."

Stuart pretended to clap. "Very impressive. Boy, the two of you make some team. I guess it's important to be practical when you always have to make a little bit go a long way."

"What's that supposed to mean?" I asked angrily.

"You know exactly what I mean," Stuart shot back. "This is probably the farthest you've ever been away from home, right? If it wasn't for my father and me you probably would've spent Easter vacation watching MTV. That is, if your mom can afford cable."

"Why are you being so obnoxious, Stuart?" Talia asked.

"Because you're no different from him," Stuart replied spitefully. "I mean, am I really supposed to believe that you would have spent Easter vacation with me if we weren't going to a resort in Mexico? Like if I invited you to spend the vacation in a trailer park in Brownsville, I'm supposed to believe you'd be packed and ready to go? Admit it, Talia, you saw this as a chance to see the world. I was just an annoying little gnat you figured you'd have to put up with along the way."

"I thought we'd have fun," Talia replied.

Stuart snorted bitterly. "Yeah, well, we're sure having a lot of fun now."

Thankfully, the conversation died. I undid a flashlight and dumped out the batteries. Then I filled the case with water and handed it to Talia.

She drank the water quickly and made a face. "Tastes like plastic."

"That's why I let you drink first," I said with a wink. I refilled the flashlight case and handed it to Stuart, who practically downed it all in one gulp. He held out the empty flashlight case. "How about a refill?"

I shook my head. "We have to conserve."

"Conserve, blerve, I'm still thirsty." Stuart shook the flashlight case at me. "Fill 'er up, Chief."

"No," I answered.

24

Stuart narrowed his eyes at me. "Know what? I'm getting really sick of you telling me what to do. Now, gimme that water."

I didn't budge. "We have a total of eight and a half quarts of drinkable water, including the Hawaiian Punch. Suppose we're stuck out here for a week? That means slightly less than a pint a day for each of us."

Stuart glanced at his father. I wondered if he was thinking that Mr. Green wasn't drinking anything and therefore didn't have to be counted. Stuart shook the flashlight at me again. "Come on, man, I'm really parched."

I knew it was a bad idea, but I figured it might just be worth it to keep the peace. I refilled the flashlight halfway. To my surprise,

Stuart accepted that without argument. Then I filled the flashlight with the same amount and handed it to my sister.

"It's only fair," I explained.

Talia accepted the flashlight and drank it down. "Thanks. I have to admit I'm really thirsty, too."

I took the flashlight back and gave myself the same amount I'd given the others.

"Tastes pretty good, huh?" Stuart asked.

I couldn't argue. The water felt great going down, and I wished I could have more. A lot more.

"How about some more?" Stuart asked.

I shook my head. "We have to conserve." Truth was, the thought of a little more water was incredibly tempting.

"Come on, Ian," Stuart urged me. "You know we're gonna get rescued in less than a week. You said it yourself. This isn't the middle of the ocean. It's the Gulf of Mexico, for Pete's sake. It's practically a big lake."

"There's no lake in the world that even comes close to the size of this," I replied.

"Yeah, yeah, don't be so literal," Stuart scoffed. "I was only trying to make a point. Now how about it? Another half a flashlight each, okay?"

I poured it out for each of us. "Maybe we'll get some rain," I said, trying to convince myself that it was okay.

"Why?" Stuart asked. "What'll we do? Stick our heads out with our mouths open?"

I pointed at the canopy. "There are rainwater collectors on the outside. We'll use them to replenish our supply."

Stuart gave me a wondrous look. "Seriously, how do you know all this stuff?"

"He reads everything he can about sailing," Talia answered.

"What are you, a sailing nut?" Stuart asked.

I felt my face grow red with embarrassment.

"Let's put it this way," Talia said. "He probably would've gone to that trailer park in Brownsville for Easter vacation. But only if you sailed there."

Stuart smirked. "Well, I hate to say it, but we're probably lucky to have him along."

"Even though I brought the sharks?" I asked.

"They probably would've come anyway," Stuart admitted.

I dried out the inside of the flashlight with a sponge I'd found in the repair kit, then put it back together. I was already regretting what we'd just done. In that one sitting we'd each consumed a whole day's ration of water. At that rate our supply wouldn't last another three days.

If it didn't rain, and we weren't rescued by then, we would begin the slow, agonizing process of death from thirst.

25

The afternoon hours passed. We took turns kneeling in the canopy opening to watch for a ship or airplane. While one of us watched, the others tried to lie down and doze. It was impossible to find a comfortable position. The rubbery surface of the raft's floor grabbed at the skin. Some of the seawater that had sloshed in earlier had dried, leaving a thin film of whitish salt that burned when it got into a sore or scrape.

"How do people sleep on waterbeds?" Talia groaned.

"With sheets and blankets," Stuart answered. It was his turn to do the watch. "I just can't believe we haven't seen another ship yet."

"I'm trying to remember the distance to the

horizon from sea level," I said. "I think it's like ten miles."

"What's that mean?" Stuart asked.

"We can only see ten miles in any direction," I explained.

"Shouldn't that be enough?" Stuart asked.

"The Gulf's a pretty big body of water," I said.

"Didn't take long for the sharks to find us," Stuart said.

I gave him a look. Was he blaming me again?

But when he saw my look, he quickly added, "Hey, I didn't mean it that way."

I nodded to let him know I understood. "They still out there?"

Stuart looked around. "Nope."

"That's a relief," Talia said with a sigh.

Stuart slumped down into the raft. "How about something to eat?"

Among the foods in plastic storage bags that Talia had been able to salvage was a box of Fig Newtons, which we managed to finish in practically no time.

"How about something to wash it down with?" Stuart asked.

It had been hours since we'd had water. Once again we were all feeling uncomfortably thirsty.

"Okay," I said, "but just a little."

Stuart groaned. "Yeah, yeah, I know. We still have to conserve."

"You want water or Hawaiian Punch?" I asked.

"Why don't we splurge with the punch?" Stuart suggested.

The can was in the pants I'd sunk off the side of the raft. I reached for the line attached to the pants and gave it a yank.

Wham! Something hit the raft from underneath so hard we nearly tipped over! I toppled backward and into Mr. Green.

"What the . . . !" Stuart yelled and Talia let out a shriek. I was reaching for one of the overhead straps to pull myself back up when . . . *Splash!* Something seemed to yank down on one side of the raft, nearly tipping it over.

Splash! Another sudden jerk sent us all tumbling. The raft kept bouncing up and down. It was like riding a bucking bronco.

Like something was trying to pull us under.

Then the raft began to move as if something was pulling it.

Suddenly I realized what it was. "The pants!" I shouted.

Having just finished his watch, Stuart was the closest to the opening in the canopy. He stuck his head out and looked down, then immediately lurched back as if he'd seen a ghost, or worse, a huge shark. The next thing I knew, Stuart reached down and yanked the diving knife out of the sheath on his calf.

"No!" I shouted.

Too late. Stuart brought the knife down hard on the line tied to the pants.

The knife blade went through the line like butter.

The raft suddenly stopped.

Shhhhhhhhh . . .

The only sounds we heard were the pounding of our hearts . . .

Our loud gasps for breath . . .

And the hiss of air escaping from the tube Stuart had accidentally slashed.

26

We sat in stunned silence as the upper tube deflated. The raft slowly sank under our weight. There was nothing we could do now. If the raft went down, we were finished.

Shark bait.

Just like Pops had said.

Sea water started to slosh over the deflated tube and into the raft. I quickly reached into the mesh and found the soft plastic bailer. I handed it to Stuart, who was still sitting closest to the canopy opening.

"Better bail," I said.

Stuart started to bail. Luckily the Gulf was calm and the lower tube had escaped Stuart's knife. Only a little water was dribbling into the raft.

"I can't believe I did that," Stuart sputtered. "I mean, I only did it because that dumb shark was pulling us. It was those stupid pants, you know. If you hadn't filled them with that stuff, the shark wouldn't have—"

"Shut up!" I exploded with a force that surprised even me. Stuart and Talia stared at me in shock.

"It's no one's fault," I fumed. "Not yours, not mine, no one's. Everyone's doing the best they can. No one knew the shark was under the raft. No one knew he'd go after the pants like that. None of us has ever been in something like this before, so we're bound to make mistakes. Just forget about it, okay? There's no point in blaming anyone. Let's just figure out what we're going to do next."

Stuart's eyes met mine. He actually looked surprised. Here was the perfect opportunity for me to get him back. To make fun of the incredibly dumb thing he'd done. And yet I wouldn't do it.

"What are we going to do next?" Talia asked.

Good question. With the upper tube deflated, seawater sloshed in the canopy opening every time someone moved. That would make it hard to watch for a ship or a plane. And if the weather changed and the waves kicked up, we'd be in serious danger of swamping.

"We have to fix the tube," I said. I started to search through the mesh until I found a repair kit. Now I had to figure out a way to do the repair. I knew that for the patch to work, the rubber around the slash had to be dry and clear of salt. But the slash in the tube was at the canopy opening where the water was sloshing in.

I turned to Stuart. "We have to move your father."

"Why?" Stuart asked.

"We have to get as much weight as possible on the back side of the raft," I explained. "If we're lucky, that'll tip the front part of the raft up and keep it dry while I patch it."

In the raft, jobs that normally would have taken minutes took much longer. With each move, water sloshed in. Now Talia had the job of bailing while Stuart and I undid the space blanket and moved Mr. Green.

"Look, I didn't mean to blame you," Stuart said sheepishly. "You're right. It's no one's fault."

I nodded. That was better. Maybe it was a good time to talk, but the problem was that the sun was going down. It would be much harder to patch the raft in the dark.

And if we had to go through the night with water sloshing in, I wasn't sure we would make it.

27

When Talia and Stuart huddled in the other end of the raft with Mr. Green, it lifted my end out of the water enough for the slashed area to dry in the waning afternoon sun. Next I had to scrape off the white dusting of salt the dried seawater had left behind.

The hardest part of the job was keeping the slashed area straight and dry while I painted on the adhesive and laid on the rubber patch. The sun was going down and it was cooler now, but drops of sweat fell from my forehead. Drops of worry and concentration, I supposed.

"I'm impressed," Stuart said as I worked. "How do you know how to do that?"

"I've patched the tube in my bike," I explained. "This is basically the same thing."

"Know what I do when one of my tires goes flat?" Stuart asked.

"Take it to the bike shop?" I guessed.

"Naw, I just buy a new bike," he said.

I gave him a questioning look.

He grinned. "You believed me, didn't you?"

"Well . . ." I hesitated.

Stuart shook his head wondrously. "I was only joking."

I did the best job I could of pressing the patch down on the deflated tube and squeezing out all the air bubbles. Now it just had to dry.

Meanwhile, the sun had become an orange orb settling down into the horizon. I guess I must've given Talia a rueful look, because she asked what I was thinking.

"One thing I was really looking forward to on this trip was seeing some nice sunsets over the water," I answered. "Guess I finally got my wish."

"Glad to be of service," Stuart said with a chuckle.

In the last gray light of dusk it was time to reinflate the raft. I searched around until I found the pump. It was a foot-bellows, the kind of pump you were supposed to step down on to force air out. Again, someone wasn't thinking straight when they'd put it in the life raft canister. There weren't any firm places to step down on when you were huddled inside a raft with a soft floor. I looked around, trying to figure out how best to use the pump.

"What's the problem?" Stuart asked.

"It's a foot pump," I explained. To demonstrate the problem, I tried to squeeze it closed with my hands. I was barely able to do it.

"I get it," Stuart said. "At that rate it'll take a week to blow up the raft."

"We need something hard to push against," I said.

"How about my head?" Stuart pointed at his skull. "Oh, no, sorry. You said hard, not thick."

Talia and I smiled. The joke was unexpected coming from Stuart. I was starting to see that he did have a sense of humor.

"Why don't you both push against it?" my sister suggested.

"Good idea." I held the pump between Stuart and myself. We both pushed against it at the same time, squeezing the bellows. Air hissed out through a hose and into the upper raft tube.

Working that way, it took about fifteen minutes to inflate the tube. It was difficult, tiring work, and Stuart and I broke out in a sweat. When the tube wouldn't take any more air I quickly sealed it. Outside, it was dark. We were about to spend our first night in the raft.

"Phew!" Stuart wiped the sweat off his brow. "Now I'm really thirsty. How about a drink?"

We'd lost the big can of Hawaiian Punch. That left the plastic jug of emergency water and the eight pint-size cans that had come with the raft.

"Listen, Stuart, seriously," I said. "We've already had more than a day's ration. At this rate we're going to run out the day after tomorrow. We have to conserve."

To my surprise, I got no argument.

28

"**A**h!" The scream shook me out of my sleep and sent me scrambling for a flashlight.

"What's going on? What happened?" Talia's worried voice asked in the dark.

I found the flashlight and flicked it on. Talia shielded her eyes against the sudden bright beam of light and shook her head. "Not me. It was Stuart."

I swung the flashlight beam at Stuart. He was breathing hard. Beads of sweat on his forehead glimmered in the flashlight beam.

"Didn't you feel it?" he gasped.

I shook my head. It was supposed to be my turn to stand watch, but I'd fallen asleep.

In the dark Stuart turned to my sister. "What about you, Talia?"

"Feel what?" Talia asked.

"Something rubbed against the bottom of the raft," Stuart said. "It was huge."

In the dark Talia and I shared a look. Neither of us had felt anything.

"I'm telling you, I felt it," Stuart insisted. "It wasn't a dream."

"No one's arguing with you," I replied. "To tell you the truth, I was asleep."

"I thought it was your watch," Stuart said.

"Yeah, well, guess I didn't do such a hot job," I admitted.

Meanwhile, Talia's eyes widened. "Look!" She pointed out the canopy opening and into the dark. I twisted around. A tiny green light was creeping along the horizon where the inky black of the sea met the starlit black of the night sky.

"Get a flare!" I urgently swept the flashlight beam around the inside of the raft until it settled on the flare kit. Stuart grabbed it. Flares of several different lengths and shapes tumbled out.

"Which one?" Stuart asked.

I looked out again. The green light was barely visible and barely moving. I suspected that it was a sailboat, and that it was very far away. I turned back to Stuart. "Does one say anything about a parachute?"

Stuart sorted through the flares and held one up. "This one."

"Great." I grabbed it. Holding the flashlight in my mouth, I quickly read the instructions. Then I held the flare out of the canopy opening and twisted it.

Whoosh! The flare shot out like a big Roman candle. High in the sky above us it burst into a bright orange ball of light and then began to float slowly back down, held aloft by a small, unseen parachute.

We watched eagerly for some sign that the faraway boat had seen the flare. Perhaps a flashing light or an answering flare.

But we saw nothing.

Meanwhile, our own flare began to dim and float back to the sea.

"Did they see it?" Stuart asked anxiously.

"If they did, they're not responding," I said glumly.

"How could they not see it?" Stuart wondered out loud.

"That boat's awfully far away," I answered. "To them our flare would just be a speck on the horizon. I hate to say it, but it could be easy to miss."

"Launch another flare," Talia said.

"How many do we have left?" I asked.

"Don't worry about that now!" Stuart cried impatiently. "Fire another!"

I launched a second parachute flare and watched the orange ball burst brightly in the sky above. I just hoped that wasn't the last parachute flare we had.

The seconds passed slowly. The flare began to dim and float back down. I kept my eye on the faraway green light. Nothing changed. The light slowly moved along the horizon.

And finally vanished.

In the raft no one said a word.

I stared up at the stars twinkling brightly in the dark night sky. I had a feeling I knew how it felt to be lost in space.

29

Our second day in the raft began as hot and still as ever. I woke to the sound of loud moaning. It woke Talia and Stuart, too. The moans were coming from Mr. Green, whose skin had turned pale. His eyes, though closed, seemed to have sunk into his skull. His lips were wrinkled and cracked.

"What do you think is wrong?" Stuart asked nervously.

I turned to Talia. "What's your guess?"

"He probably hasn't had a drop of water in three days," she answered.

"He's been unconscious," Stuart said.

"He still needs water," Talia said.

"What do we do?" Stuart asked.

"Let's sit him up and try to get some into him," my sister suggested.

Stuart and I undid the space blanket and managed to prop up Mr. Green's head. As I leaned against the raft's wall, I noticed that the lower tube felt soft and spongy. Meanwhile, Talia poured some water into the flashlight case.

"Real gently and slowly," she cautioned as she poured a tiny bit of water into Mr. Green's mouth.

Stuart's father didn't respond. Talia gave us a worried look.

"Try a little more," I suggested.

Talia poured a little more water into Mr. Green's mouth, and then a little more.

Suddenly Mr. Green coughed violently. Talia was caught by surprise and dropped the flashlight. Precious water spilled on the floor of the raft.

"It's useless," Stuart complained.

"Let's try again," Talia said. "I thought he actually swallowed some."

She poured more water into the flashlight and once again dripped a little into Mr. Green's mouth. This time I was certain I saw Mr. Green's Adam's apple move up and down.

"He definitely swallowed," I said.

But the words were hardly out of my mouth when Stuart's father coughed again. For a second time the water in the flashlight spilled to the raft's floor.

"I'm sorry," Talia apologized as she picked up the flashlight. "I really didn't expect him to cough again. It caught me off guard."

"You don't have to apologize," Stuart said.

Talia looked at him for a moment, then smiled slightly as if she appreciated it. "Okay, thanks."

A gurgling sound came from Mr. Green. It sounded like there was still some water caught in his throat. Then he swallowed again, and the gurgling sound stopped.

"Well, the good news is he's getting some of it," I said.

"You want to try again?" Talia asked.

"This is costing us a lot of water," Stuart said.

"What choice do we have?" I asked.

Stuart turned to Talia. "Just hold that flashlight tight."

With a lot of coughing and gurgling from Mr. Green, we managed to get about a pint of water down his throat. Meanwhile, another pint wound up on the floor of the raft. Now the plastic water jug was almost empty. We were running out.

After we got Mr. Green back into the space blanket, I turned and pressed my finger against the raft's tubes. This time the others watched. The upper tube felt firm and resisted the pressure. But my finger sank easily into the black rubber of the lower tube.

"It's leaking, isn't it?" Stuart said solemnly.

"Yes," I answered.

30

We spent most of the morning searching for the leak, but couldn't find it. For a while Stuart and I were able to keep the lower tube inflated by pumping in more air with the bellows, but the leak was getting worse. Soon the air was leaving as fast as we could pump it in. Stuart kept pushing against the bellows without complaint, but sweat was dripping down both his and my foreheads.

"I don't get it," I said. "If we're losing that much air we should be able to see or hear the leak."

"It could be behind us or on the bottom of the raft," Talia suggested. "Even if we found it, we might not be able to patch it."

I knew she was right, but when Stuart and

I stopped pumping, the raft began to settle down to the top tube. Once again any false move resulted in sea water splashing in.

And the long dark shadows were back, circling the raft.

It almost seemed as if they knew something was wrong and sensed that the opportunity to eat was near.

To make things worse, a breeze had kicked up, creating waves. They were just big enough to splash seawater into the raft through the canopy opening. Overhead the sky turned gray as thick clouds rolled in.

"Now what?" Stuart asked as the seawater spilled into the raft, making us all wet and uncomfortable.

"We have to figure out a way to keep the water out," I said, then picked up the soft plastic bailer and started to bail.

"Maybe we could tape something across the bottom of the opening," Talia suggested.

"Do we have tape?" I asked.

"In the first-aid kit," answered my sister. "Adhesive."

I wasn't sure the adhesive tape would hold against the salt water, but anything was worth a try. Once again Talia and Stuart sat with Mr. Green on the opposite side of the raft to help lift the side I was working on out of the water.

After cutting a piece of the space blanket to use as a barrier, I started to tape it to the top edge of the tube. But it had begun to drizzle outside, making it difficult to keep the tube dry.

"You have that sponge?" I asked.

Stuart handed me the sponge. As I leaned in the opening of the canopy and worked, I tried to hide my concerns from the others. The wind was picking up, and the drizzle was turning to rain. The waves were starting to crest. If I couldn't get this barrier to work, it wouldn't be long before the raft was swamped.

I concentrated on the job, first drying a small spot on the tube, then quickly putting down a piece of tape and sticking the other end to the space-blanket barrier. I was so focused I virtually blocked out everything that was happening around me.

So I never noticed the long, dark shadow gliding quietly toward us in the water.

31

When the sea just outside the canopy opening exploded, I had no idea what hit us. With a loud splash something knocked me clear across the raft and into Mr. Green. Talia screamed. Stuart's father let out a loud groan. Gallons of seawater splashed into the raft.

The raft began to lurch right and left as if something was trying to tear it apart from below.

"What the . . . !" Stuart cried out as he smashed his forehead into my knee. "Ow!"

"Shark!" I yelled and tried to grab one of the straps hanging from the canopy.

Stuart was holding his forehead. Bright red blood started to gush out between his fingers. The gash had reopened when he'd banged into me.

The raft shook again. A vision of what was happening flashed into my mind. I'd seen enough nature shows to know that after biting into their prey, sharks often jerked side to side in an attempt to tear off large chunks. I could imagine the huge shark beneath us with its jaw clamped on the bottom of the raft.

Riiipppp! A muffled, watery ripping sound came from under the raft.

A split second later it stopped lurching.

"What happened?" Talia gasped.

"I don't know," I answered, looking around anxiously to see if the raft had survived the attack. It was hard to tell because the raft was half swamped. We were sitting in six inches of water now. Cans of emergency water, flares, and plastic bags floated around us.

We heard a gurgling sound. Mr. Green's face was half-submerged!

"Get his head up before he drowns!" Talia cried.

We were propping up Mr. Green's head when something hit the raft again, this time from underneath. The floor rose up from below, and we could actually feel the hard, rounded snout of the shark under us.

Thunk! Stuart grabbed an emergency water

can and smashed it down as hard as he could on the shark's snout. To my surprise, the shark actually sank back.

Stuart and I shared a stunned look. Then he grinned and raised his hand.

Slap! I gave him a high five. He deserved it.

But our smiles quickly faded. The raft was now awash. Seawater flowed in and out over the partly submerged tube. Amazingly, the tube appeared to still be inflated, but I watched helplessly as a flare and one of the cans of emergency water floated out of the opening before any of us could grab it.

Stuart was still holding his forehead. Blood and seawater ran over his hands and down his arms to his elbows, where it dripped off.

The bloody seawater washed over the tube and out of the raft.

Thrash! We watched in shock as a shark broke the water not five feet from the raft and swallowed the emergency water can. Excited by the blood, dark shadows were rocketing through the water in all directions.

"My Lord!" Talia cried.

I started scooping up the cans and flares floating in the raft. "Get the rest of this stuff before it washes out!"

Talia started to help with one hand while keeping Mr. Green's head out of the water with the other. Stuart picked up the flare pistol and slid in one of the meteor flares.

"What are you doing?" I asked.

"No sense waiting to use these now!" Stuart yelled back and aimed the pistol out of the canopy opening.

"Wait!" I shouted. I thought I heard something.

"No way!" Stuart shouted. "What's the point?"

"Listen!" I yelled.

Stuart went quiet. We could hear a faint, faraway thumping sound. In a flash Stuart and I stuck our heads out of the canopy. Off in the distance a dark spot appeared against the gray clouds.

Whum-pid-uh-whum-pid-uh-whum-pid-uh . . .

Now I recognized the thumping sound.

"A helicopter!" I shouted.

Stuart stared at me, slack-jawed. "What should I do?"

"Fire that thing!" I yelled.

Phump! Stuart pointed the flare pistol out of the opening and pulled the trigger. The meteor flare shot high in the air and glowed bright red. He ejected the spent cartridge and started to load another. In the meantime I grabbed the last remaining parachute flare.

I was about to fire it when Talia screamed.

I looked out of the canopy. A huge shark was barreling straight toward us with its jaws open. We could actually see its teeth.

32

Without thinking, I aimed the parachute flare at the shark and fired.

Phwaaammmp! A huge orange glow burst in our faces. The raft filled with acrid orange smoke. Our eyes were burning and all of us began coughing on the orange chemicals filling the air.

Where was the shark?

Hiiiissss! I could hear air escaping from the tube. The stink of burning rubber hit my nose. The parachute flare must have ricocheted off the shark. It was burning into the raft!

The water level was rising higher!

We were splashing around. I couldn't feel the floor of the raft anymore!

Through the orange smoke I caught a

glimpse of Stuart. His face and hair were smeared with orange chemicals. His eyes were round with fright, and he was still holding the flare pistol.

"We're sinking!" I shouted.

Thrash! A sudden huge splash broke the water between us!

It was the shark!

33

Its mouth was open, row after row of pointed sharp teeth bared. But its snout and head were streaked with the orange chemicals from the parachute flare. It thrashed its head back and forth blindly, churning the water between Stuart and me into an orange-tinted froth.

"Shoot it!" I shouted at Stuart.

Stuart looked at the pistol in his hand as if he'd forgotten it was there.

Then he aimed it into the shark's mouth and pulled the trigger.

Bang! The meteor flare fired.

Snap! The shark slammed his huge jaws shut.

Whump! I heard a dull, thudding explosion.

The next thing we knew, the shark slid backward and disappeared below the surface.

WHUM-PID-UH-WHUM-PID-UH-WHUM-PID-UH . . . The sound of the helicopter was loud and right overhead now.

A second later the surface of the water around us was whipped into a frenzy by the rotors above. Shielding my eyes from the spray, I quickly spun around to look for the others. Floating around me were emergency water cans and deflated raft debris. A slick of orange chemicals floated on the water's surface.

And there was Stuart . . . Talia . . . Mr. Green. . . .

We were all there, bobbing in the water in our bright orange life vests, our hair and faces smeared with orange chemicals.

But where were the sharks?

34

"*Get the sling!*" The shout from above caught me by surprise. I looked up at the white-and-orange Coast Guard helicopter hovering above us. Two helmeted crewmen were lowering a bright yellow U-shaped rescue sling on a cable.

I grabbed the sling and swam toward Mr. Green. Stuart joined me, and together we managed to get his father's head and arms through it.

"Lift!" I shouted up at the crewmen.

The cable went tight, and Mr. Green, dripping, limp, and unconscious, began to rise out of the water.

Pow! The crack of a rifle shot made me jump. A dozen yards away the water exploded

139

as the huge, orange-streak shark jerked spasmodically.

I looked up at the helicopter. One of the crewmen was kneeling in the bay with a rifle in his hands. Smoke curled from the rifle's barrel.

But what about the other sharks?

They couldn't be far away.

In the helicopter bay the crewmen pulled Mr. Green out of the sling. It seemed to be taking them forever.

Come on, guys! I thought. We don't have all day!

35

Finally the sling came back down. We helped Talia into it.

A few moments later Stuart went up.

When the sling finally came back down, I slid my arms through it and felt myself being lifted out of the water. Below me the orange-and-black deflated raft bobbed on the surface. The chemical slick from the parachute flare was breaking up into patches of blue and orange. About twenty yards away half a dozen dark torpedo shapes thrashed and fought in the water, kicking up reddish foam.

What were they feeding on?

I kept rising in the air. Soon I felt hands on my shoulders and arms. Next I felt the hard floor of the helicopter against my back as I was pulled on board.

"You okay?" one of the helmeted crewmen yelled at me.

"I think so!" I yelled back. I craned my neck around the bay. Talia was wrapped in a blanket. She smiled back at me. A crewman was crouched over Stuart, wrapping his head with gauze. Not far from me, Mr. Green lay strapped in a gurney.

We were all safe.

As the helicopter tilted and began to go, I looked back down. Below, the dark shapes of the sharks swirled and fought.

Suddenly, in the middle of the thrashing reddish water, the head of the huge, orange-streaked shark bobbed up. His mouth was half open and his lifeless eyes stared up at me, as if he couldn't understand why his companions were feeding on him and not us.

A split-second later he sank away.

36

"**M**an, I wish you'd seen it," Stuart was telling Talia as we waited outside Mr. Green's room in the hospital in Brownsville. All three of us had been checked out in the emergency room, but only Mr. Green had to be admitted to the hospital.

Stuart's head was bandaged, but it didn't seem to bother him as he went into a police crouch with his hands together, pretending he was aiming a pistol. "That big sucker was coming at me and *Pow!* I got him right in the mouth with the meteor flare."

Talia stared at him with a wondrous look on her face.

Stuart grinned proudly. "It must've burned

his throat out. Those other sharks were on him in an instant. I saved our lives."

Talia gave me a quizzical look as if asking if that was what had really happened. I winked back. It was easy to imagine that in the midst of all the excitement Stuart never heard the helicopter crewman's rifle shot.

The door opened and a doctor wearing a bright blue Hawaiian shirt came out.

"What's the story, Doc?" Stuart asked.

"He's got a pretty bad concussion and he's dehydrated," the doctor reported. "I'd like to keep him here for a couple of days. But he'll be okay."

"Can I see him?" Stuart asked.

The doctor shook his head. "He's resting now. Why don't you wait until later?"

"Sure thing," said Stuart.

The doctor left.

Stuart turned to Talia and me. "What are you going to do?"

"I guess we'll wire our mom for the bus fare home," Talia said with a shrug.

Stuart stared down at the floor for a moment. I thought he looked disappointed. Then he looked up and grinned.

"Hey," he said. "We're in swinging Brownsville, right? Suppose I get us a couple of motel rooms and we have some fun while we wait for my dad to get out of the hospital?"

Talia gave me another questioning look. I answered with a nod. I'd been wrong about Stuart. He was an okay guy.

My sister turned back to Stuart.

"Sure," she said with a smile. "Why not?"

ABOUT THE AUTHOR

Todd Strasser has written many award-winning novels for young and teenage readers. Among his best known books are those in the *Help! I'm Trapped In . . .* series. Todd speaks frequently at schools about the craft of writing and conducts writing workshops for young people. He and his wife, children, and Labrador retriever live in a suburb of New York. Todd and his family enjoy boating, hiking, and mountain climbing.